Love's Return

Dedicated to our war veterans and their families

Deborah Laurel

Thanks to all our Service men + women + families

Love's Return is not a "run of the mill" book for those who love romance novels, but serves a great purpose and need. Deborah Tainsh skillfully weaves the agony of PTSD (Post Traumatic Stress Disorder) through the story with realistic characters in a way that touches readers' hearts with truths about some of the struggles of our returning war veterans.

As a retired librarian I've read hundreds of books. I categorize writing as good, jagged (not a very good flow), or excellent. Written from a perspective known by few, Deborah's writing is excellent and flows smoothly, causing a reader to "get lost" in the story and the landscape of her beautiful and historical home town of Panama City Beach, Florida.

> -Margaret True, Bay County, Florida Librarian (Ret)
> Panama City Beach, Florida

"Love's Return is a beautiful love story! A veteran dealing with PTSD while trying to be a good dad and son has so much reality in it. The historical aspects of Panama City Beach, Florida made me feel like I have been there, or certainly can't wait to get there!! What a great book!"

> -Kathleen Mahardy, Mom of a war veteran
> Syracuse, New York

"I couldn't wait to turn the pages of this love story and follow the journey of the characters that were all too real to me!"

> -Meghan Mahardy, Wife of a war veteran
> USArmy, Belgium

"Deborah's "word smith" ability created a page turner with unforgettable characters that brought out every emotion from laughter to tears while reminding readers about the struggles of our war veterans."

> -Colleen Greene, Mom of a war veteran
> Panama City, Florida

ACKNOWLEDGEMENTS

I've heard it said that the best stories come by way of "the things or people we are most familiar with." Through the years of war in Iraq and Afghanistan and as the widow of a United States Marine Vietnam Veteran who passed away in 2014 from lung cancer attributed to agent-orange, I have been privileged to meet some of the most courageous and determined individuals anyone could come to know. The courageous make up the military personnel who "signed a blank check" to serve and defend without question each one of us and others abroad. The courageous are also the families of those who serve and remain behind on one shore while their loved ones walk into the face of danger on others. Together, service members and their families work with determination for the healing of souls of so much pain acquired in the aftermath of war.

Although *Love's Return* is my first work of fiction with characters set in my home town of Panama City Beach, Florida, the military family issues dealt with in the book are very real.

This page will not hold the names of everyone that I have shared both pain and triumphs with along our journey as military families since 9/11. As the mom of a soldier killed in action in Baghdad, Iraq in 2004, there are those who have blessed me richly. Among those are special names whose friendship and lives gave rise in my heart for *Love's Return*.

Stacey, Jim, Chris, Adam, Ron, Matthew, Joe, &
special moms and friends, Kathy and Colleen.

To my dear friends, Nancy, Sherri, Kathy, Meghan, Debbie & Margaret who read the manuscript as I put it together piece by piece. I can't thank you enough for your input and encouragement to bring the manuscript to book form. Dan C., thank you for input as an EMT. Thanks Katie C. for the stories of Wisconsin and cows.

To soul sister, Colleen Greene, mom of a United States Marine who served two tours in Afghanistan, thank you for the hours you spent reading, editing and sitting with me to make this a completed work, that although fiction, reflects difficulties that our military war veterans and families face.

It is courage

that raises the blood of life to crimson splendor.

Live bravely and present a brave front to adversity!

- Horace

PROLOGUE
Spring, 2009

"Dustin, wake up," Maxie Brites called to her son from the doorway to his bedroom. "Son, you're at home. No one is outside the window. No one is in danger."

"No, they're out there in the dark. I see them. They're planting an explosive device on the road. I've got to stop them before one of our vehicles runs over it and kills everyone."

"Dustin," Maxie called louder. "It's Mom. I'm here. We're all okay. Your dad and Shay are safe. You can go back to bed now. There's no danger. I promise."

Dustin stared through the window a few more moments before turning and walking back toward his bed. The sheets were drenched with sweat. Before he could lie down, Maxie asked softly, "Dustin, are you awake now?" Maxie didn't dare touch Dustin while he was still sleep-walking. Doing that could cause injury to them both.

"Mom?"

"Yes, Son. I'm here."

"Mom, I'm sorry. I'm so sorry. I couldn't save the men I was responsible for. I was their medic and I couldn't save them. Will I ever feel better?"

"Yes, Son, you will. For now, let's get you to the guest room into a bed with dry sheets."

After Dustin was settled, Maxie sat down in the chair in the corner of the room. Both awake, mother and son talked until sunrise. Dustin cried. And Maxie's heart almost burst with pain because she had no answer when her son said: "Mom, I tried, I tried so hard to save them. Why did I get to come back home and they didn't? I don't deserve to be here.

CHAPTER ONE

June 1, 2011

At the outdoor shower by the city pier in Panama City Beach, Florida, twenty-nine year old Dustin Brites sprayed the sea salt from his kayak and then let the cool water flow down his long athletic body. He ran his fingers through his short dark hair as he carried the kayak to his old beloved pick-up truck. He'd had the mode of transportation since he was nineteen when he bought it from his dad on installment payments, and never cared to have a newer one. Tinkering with the engine or sanding it for a new paint job was a good hobby, especially now as a combat veteran that often needed distractions from war memories.

After securing the kayak inside the truck bed, Dustin picked up the t-shirt that lay on the seat and pulled it over his head, turned the engine and headed home. The high season Sunday traffic moved at thirty-five miles per hour along Front Beach Road. People came from every state in the union to Panama City Beach, a part of the Florida Panhandle one hundred miles east of Pensacola, home of the National Naval Air Museum and the Navy's *Blue Angels*.

The greatest number of visitors came from the nearest southern states. People from outside the South were always amused to learn that the pet name for this area along the Gulf of Mexico was *Redneck Riviera*. Fun loving southerners had coined the term decades ago.

They treasured the coastline's wind-swept dunes that clutched tall grasses and sea oats that swayed back and forth on warm breezes, and the emerald water's gentle surf that massaged the shore's sugar-white sand. A barefoot stroll in the soft beach sand in search of sea shells and sand dollars was a family affair. And come evening, eyes and cameras turned toward the sunsets that left pink, lavender and red hues painted across pale blue sky. The *Redneck Riviera* captured souls in only the most wonderful ways. Once there, visitors found it difficult to leave and return to the mundane.

In recent years community leaders had worked diligently to transform the once secret and quiet beach community into upscale condominiums and vacation homes for the well-to-do from around and outside the USA. Commercial buildings replaced acres of sand pines, laurel oaks, and saw palmettos. So *Redneck Riviera* was not a term embraced by city officials and definitely not appropriate for marketing materials. There was hope that with time the southern term of endearment would fade away like that of Miracle Strip, now best known as Front Beach Road. The former name had come from the Miracle Strip Amusement Park built in 1963 and closed in September, 2004. Anyone new to the community would never know that the current empty piece of earth across from the beach at the corner of Alf Coleman and Front Beach Road held forty years of memories not only for locals, but for thousands of tourists, spring breakers and young lovers that had visited. The amusement park's cacophony of sounds and numerous colored lights had bounced off the night sky and created magic for young and old alike.

Dustin, his sister, and school friends could only reminisce about their favorite arcade games, the beloved wooden Starliner rollercoaster, a classic merry-go-round, and other rides for every age that had been sent elsewhere. Dustin's mother often recalled how his father had proposed marriage to her at the top of the Ferris wheel on a night when a full moon created a lighted path that rippled across the Gulf of Mexico.

The amusement park had been removed for the sake of another potential high rise condominium which had not yet come to fruition. The former piece of paradise was now nothing more than a parking lot.

Dustin was born in Bay County and raised on the beach side of Hathaway Bridge that crossed the bay and separated Panama City from Panama City Beach. He vaguely remembered when mostly mom and pop hotels were strung along the beach shores and a room cost much less than a hundred dollars per night. A few were left, but with time they would sell. Cars could once drive directly onto the beach before restrictions commenced for building condominiums along the miles of sugar white sand. Now it was getting more difficult to see the natural beauty of the emerald water, sand dunes, and sea oats while driving down Front Beach Road. But even with so much change in his twenty-nine years, for all the places in the world Dustin had experienced, this was his paradise for living, working, and playing.

Dustin slowed for a stop light and turned up the radio volume for one of his favorite country artists. With time he had learned to relax better while driving and not become overly agitated or anxious from unexpected loud noises and traffic jams. He had worked diligently to reintegrate back into his community and family after separating from the Army with multiple tours to Afghanistan and Iraq beneath his belt. He felt fortunate to be a veteran that had returned home and after some time acquire a job that he loved with Beach Fire and Rescue.

As a teen and while attending junior college he worked summers as a beach lifeguard. He was already one with the water by the time he was six, and only became stronger and swifter through each birthday, practice and natural ability. He was on his way toward Olympic trials when 9-11 occurred. His mom and dad couldn't change his twenty year old mind when he informed them he was enlisting. Nor could Anna, his girlfriend since tenth grade. She had decided she wouldn't be a good fit for military life after their separation during boot camp and Dustin's first deployment to Afghanistan. Heart-broken, but not in spirit, Dustin placed his full attention into becoming the best Army medic possible. For those he helped to live, he was grateful for their recoveries and the fact that the number saved outweighed the losses. He had even saved an enemy combatant. Even though Dustin was a medic, he carried a weapon and shot the man to defend himself when his squad was ambushed on Thanksgiving night, 2004. But those he couldn't save remained each day in a corner of his heart and mind. Dustin kept their names forever stamped in his memory and engraved on bracelets that he kept in a special box lined with purple velvet. No, he would never forget a single name of those good men.

Kerra Masters relaxed beneath a beach umbrella that helped to protect her fair skin from the glaring sun. She was new to the area, but already familiar with the necessity of a beach umbrella and sun-block high in SPF. Without one or both of these, a fair skinned person was apt to receive extreme burns before they realized it because of the sun's strong reflection off the white sand of the Gulf Coast beaches.

Although known for its summer heat and humidity, Kerra had fallen in love with Panama City Beach after vacationing at the area's pristine beaches a year before. She and her mom drove from Wisconsin after making their choice from reading internet pages. After the last freezing Wisconsin winter and needing a fresh change in her life, Kerra had used her savings and changed residency in May. Waiting to acquire a full time job in her profession as a dental hygienist, she waited tables at a popular beach side restaurant.

But at the moment she was thinking about how embarrassing it had been to chase down her umbrella a while ago after a sharp wind gust pulled it from the sand and almost smacked a man in the head. With one hand gripping his kayak, he had raised the other and slapped away the multi-colored beach-umbrella before it struck him. When Kerra approached him to apologize and retrieve the flying nuisance, she couldn't help but notice the taut muscles in his arms, chest and abdomen. In the afternoon sun, he seemed to sparkle with drops of water from the Gulf of Mexico still clinging to his bronzed skin and dark hair. His sense of humor amused and embarrassed her when he said: "My plan of the day wasn't death by a flying beach umbrella."

"I am so sorry." Kerra couldn't say the words enough. "I thought it was deep enough in the sand."

"No harm, no foul," he replied. "Where are you digging in? I'll show you a trick that'll just about ensure you won't have to chase down your umbrella again, that is unless strong tropical winds sweep through."

"Thanks. I'm over here near the boardwalk."

Dustin followed her, fighting to ignore her slight curves, and long, lean legs that flowed from the bright orange one piece swimsuit. At Kerra's beach chair, he placed the kayak on the sand and gently took the umbrella from her. When their hands touched, an unexpected surge alarmed them both, but they kept the feeling to themselves. Dustin placed the pointed end of the umbrella post into the sand and began pushing it back and forth to create a small cavern for sand to fall into. With enough of the post buried, he packed the sand tight around it.

"There, that should keep your umbrella from becoming a danger to other beach goers," he said with a grin that showed perfectly aligned white teeth.

"Again, I'm so sorry. I appreciate the instruction. I won't forget it."

"Don't!" Dustin laughed as he picked up his kayak and walked away.

While settling herself in the beach chair to read a magazine, Kerra heard the man's voice from a few yards away.

"Hey, if you're new to the area, I hope you enjoy your visit here. There's a lot to see and do. We're known for having the world's most beautiful beaches. And if you like hiking, we have a beautiful environmental conservation park not far from here."

Kerra thanked Dustin and told him she would keep the information in mind. But before she could ask his name, the bronze, muscular stranger disappeared from sight.

"Oh well," she thought, "maybe I'll run into him again sometime."

For an hour Kerra perused her magazine while waiting for the sunset. As the sun grew to resemble a large orange ball that glowed and slid slowly behind the horizon, she pulled her camera from the beach bag. One of her favorite past times was taking sequential photos as the sun made its departure from her part of the world to enter another. Once the sun disappeared, Kerra captured an evening sky splattered with red, pink, and lavender hues woven into blue.

With enough photos for her facebook page, Kerra pulled a shirt on over her swimsuit, gathered her beach items, and joined others leaving the sugar sand and calm waters lapping at the shore.

Ten minutes after leaving the beach, Dustin pulled into his driveway. Before both feet landed on the concrete, he heard the voice that had become his solid purpose in life.

"Hey Daddy! You're finally home!"

"Hey Buddy." Dustin took a wide step forward and grabbed his son, Shay.

"Swing me around Daddy! Swing me!"

Dustin held the four year old by his wrists and brought the boy's feet off the ground as he rotated twice in a circle.

"Okay, you two, that's enough. Dinner's ready. Get washed up."

"Well Buddy, you hear the boss lady. Gammie says its chow time."

Dustin reached his arm around his mom's shoulders and pulled her closer for a hug. "And beautiful lady, how was your afternoon?"

"A bag of hoots as always!" said Maxie Brites. "That young one keeps me young and exhausted at the same time."

"You're the one that insisted on keeping him one more year before kindergarten. I could have placed him in pre-k school."

"Oh no! I can teach him more than any pre-k school! He's already reading and counting above most kids his age."

"You're the best, Mom," Dustin said, with deep affection falling into his mother's eyes. "We're the luckiest to have you care so much."

"Well, I can't think of anything else I'd rather be doing since I have the time. I may be old, but I'm not dead. Reading and counting with Shay probably helps keep my few brain cells alive. Besides, I taught you and your sister at home and I didn't do too shabby. And Shay can be more entertaining and talkative than your dad is when he's at home."

Dustin laughed and opened the door to enter the house for dinner.

Just as Kerra crossed the threshold into the beach rental cottage, her cell phone rang. She dropped the beach bag to the floor and pressed the answer button.

"Hi Mom! How's it going?"

"All's the same here at the farm. The question is how's it going for you?"

"Everything's fantastic. I just walked in from working on my tan and reading my favorite magazine at the beach. Did you know that as your middle child, researchers suspect that I had a uniquely adaptable position in the family?"

Kerra turned on a couple of lamps and flopped down on the sofa in the tropically decorated living room that opened to a small kitchen.

"Oh, is that right?" replied Sylvia Masters.

"Yep, that's what they wrote, along with that because I was the middle child I was able to learn from my older sibling and teach the younger.

"Well, I suppose that makes sense. What magazine are you reading?"

"My favorite, *Woman's World*. But here's the most important part: because I played different roles as I grew up I gained my *sharp intelligence* and *great* people skills."

Both mother and daughter laughed. "Yes, my middle child, you are one of a kind, and often under suspicion that you were switched at birth before we left the hospital. Your extreme independence has always given me and your dad concern."

"I know, I know. I've been hearing that since I was old enough to understand its meaning."

"Well, just remember you're alone in a place with no family. Have you made any friends yet?"

"No one I'd call a friend. Just acquaintances from the restaurant. I've had dinner a few times with my landlord and her husband, who, by the way, tell me I can call them 24/7 if I need anything or run into any problems."

"Let them know how much I appreciate their looking out for you."

"I will, Mom. Hey, I hope you'll visit so you can meet them and see this neat cottage where I'm living at the beach."

"I'm talking with your dad about a trip. But you know how he is. He doesn't want to leave the farm in the hands of anybody else."

"Yep, I know. But you can come."

"Honey, you know I'll get there with or without your dad. I just don't know when yet. Have you met any interesting guys at the restaurant or on the beach?"

"MOM! *For pete's sake*! I just got here! And besides, you know I've already told you that having a man in my life is not a priority for me. But to feed your curiosity, the closet encounter at the beach was today when my beach umbrella blew away in a wind gust and almost smacked some guy in the head. He was around my age and handsome. I was so utterly embarrassed. But usually being as handsome as he was also means a large ego."

Kerra emphasized the words *large ego.*

Sylvia laughed. She knew that Kerra would continue to find reasons to keep men at arm's length. She had once said, "Mom, if I get attached to a man, then I'll lose focus on what I want to achieve for myself before I settle down. People go through many changes over time. I want to discover who I really am before I have to figure out someone else."

Such was the way of Miss Independent who was always reading to learn how to best traverse her way through the journey of life. But Sylvia also knew that her daughter now tried to hide a deeper reason for not wanting to meet a man that she could love and accept love in return. All she could do was continue to pray that her middle daughter, who had become full of questions for the universe, would let go of feeling that she didn't deserve to love or be loved since the accident Kerra was in with her best friend two years ago.

"You know Mom, I hate to cut this short, but I start the new job tomorrow at the dentist office. Gotta get a shower and press my uniform. Then cozy into my pillow for a good night's sleep. I want to be energized for my new adventure in the morning."

"Alright, hon. Give me a call later in the week and let me know how the new job goes. Sweet dreams."

"Sure thing, Mom. I love you."

"I love you, too. Good night."

Kerra slept well. After the alarm sounded, she lay for a couple minutes before brushing her teeth and getting positioned on her yoga mat. Recent life challenges had taught her how helpful yoga and meditation were. The daily routine kept her feeling positive, strong and healthy. A cup of hot black tea, some fruit, and half a wheat bagel followed. While sitting on the small patio of the cottage and finishing her tea, her cell phone chirped. The text message from her mom said, "Wishing you a great day! Love you!" Kerra smiled and returned to the bedroom where she dressed and pulled her auburn hair into a pony tail. She brushed her teeth for the second time, flossed, and put on minimal makeup.

"Okay, girlie, let's get going. It's a new day for a new adventure!"

Kerra arrived at Smith and Young's dental office at 8:30 a.m. The first patients arrived at 9:00 a.m. The office served adults' and children's dental needs. This had placed Kerra at the top of the list for most qualified among a number of applicants. On the day of the final interview and being hired, she had spent a few hours at the office making acquaintance with the office staff and other hygienists. She believed this was going to be a wonderful place to spend her days.

"Good morning. Welcome to your first day at Smith & Young's!" Receptionist Sarah Henderson greeted Kerra with her sincere enthusiasm.

"Thank you. I'm excited to be here. How is the day looking?"

"Actually, not bad. Come with me and I'll reacquaint you with the break room." Kerra followed Sarah and as they entered the room she heard the staff in unison say, "Welcome Kerra!" A Welcome Kerra sign hung on the wall and coffee, hot tea, donuts and bagels waited.

"Oh, WOW! Thank you. Gosh, you all really know how to make a newbie feel at home. I guess southern hospitality isn't a fallacy!"

After everyone poured a cup of coffee or made a cup of tea, a brief meeting ensued to get the week started. Both Dr. Smith and Young arrived just before 9:00 a.m. and warmly welcomed Kerra to her first day.

At 9:00 Sarah unlocked the doors and greeted patients. They drifted to various chairs in the waiting room where walls displayed seaside art by local artists. Some picked up magazines and others cast their eyes on the news of the day that scrolled across the bottom of the television. A few patients that knew each other struck up conversations.

Along with her light blue cotton pants, a white smock covered with toothbrushes, and comfortable Sketchers, Kerra wore a welcoming smile and demeanor when she walked to the door of the waiting room.

"Good morning everyone. Is Mrs. Maxie Brites here?"

"I'm here," said the petite brunette with a few streaks of gray, who popped up from the chair like a spring. "And ready to get this over with."

Wearing knee length red shorts with white star fish, a white sleeveless top, flip-flops, and carrying a purse decorated with sea life, Maxie followed Kerra to the treatment room and took a seat in the dental chair.

"Mrs. Brites, I'm Kerra. I'll be doing your cleaning this morning. Then Dr. Smith will be in to say hello and take a quick look."

"I've never seen you before," Maxie said with a pleasant smile.

"Actually today is my first day with Smith & Young," Kerra explained as she put on medical gloves and took a seat on the stool next to Maxie.

"You're not a student fresh out of school are you? I've always had an experienced hygienist work on me. I don't mean to offend you. But my teeth and gums are just so sensitive. I'm particular about who puts those tools inside my mouth."

Kerra patted Maxie on the arm and smiled. "I promise you Mrs. Brites, I finished school a few years ago. And I've never had anyone scream or try to have me fired because I hurt them."

"Okay, I'm going to hold you to that. But where did you work before?"

"Wisconsin."

"Wisconsin! How long have you been here in our neck of the woods?"

"Almost two months now."

"And what brought you way down here? Family?"

"No. All my family is in Augusta, Wisconsin, a few hundred miles from Milwaukee. I just wanted a change. And after a vacation here last year, I decided it was the place for me to add a new chapter to my life. But for now, if you'll open wide for me, I'll take a look and get you out of here in a jiffy.

Maxie stopped the questions and relaxed in the chair for Kerra to get started. She examined the young woman's pretty face that was near the shape of a heart, clear and fresh as dew. Her hazel-blue almond shaped eyes with lashes to die for stood out with minimal eyeliner and mascara. Without bangs, her long ponytail full of sheen fell partially over one shoulder. She spoke with a gentle yet confident tone. And her smile, well, from where Maxie sat, those teeth definitely belonged to a dental hygienist.

CHAPTER TWO

Dustin Brites worked twenty-four on and forty-eight off with Beach Fire and Rescue. He reported in at 6:00 a.m. this morning. On his days off, he spent time with Shay and exercised with water sports and weights as a part of his regime to keep himself in shape for his job and to manage health and emotional issues left over from the battlefields. He also spent time on the up keep required on his parent's aging home. They had lived at the same location from before he and his sister were born.

Now back at the station, it was time for his shift to inspect the fire, EMT, and rescue trucks and prepare for any calls that came to help beach goers or locals. In summer the calls were more numerous because no matter that the warning flags might be indicating hazard, tourists often ignored them.

"Mornin' Brites. Ready for another fun day in paradise?"

Dustin cast a grin at his co-worker who was headed for home.

"You bet, Lefty. That's my motto, Toujours Pret, Always Ready." Dustin's co-workers learned after he came on board that the Toujours Pret term came from serving with the Army's Second Cavalry Regiment. A silver Fleur de Leis, the symbol of that unit, hung from a chain on the rearview mirror of his truck along with his dog tags.

"Anything interesting happen around here last night I haven't heard about yet?" Dustin asked.

"Nothing more than usual and nothing too serious. Just kids on a rental scooter not being careful. Had to take a girl and her boyfriend to the ER after he lost control in a curve. How bout you? Anything fun on your days off?"

"Just some painting on my folk's house. Took Shay to Gulf World. You know how he is about the dolphin show. Then I took an afternoon jaunt on the kayak."

"Man, when you gonna get a woman for your life?" Lefty asked as he rinsed out the coffee cup he'd been drinking from.

Dustin poured himself a cup of coffee. "Don't think I have enough time left for that.You know most women want or need more time from a man than I have to give. I love my job and hours. I have a son to care for and my folks need my support. They've done a lot for me and Shay. I owe it to them."

"I hear you." Lefty dried his hands on a paper towel and then tossed it in the trash. "Hey, I'm outta here. Hope it's a good day around here. See you later."

Dustin sipped on his cup of black coffee and opened the newspaper that was on the table. He quickly perused the sports page, followed by the outdoors section. Gag grouper season was opening soon. Gag was a big fish fun to fight with extra heavy fishing line and hooks, and live bait. They were bottom dwellers known to school in harems where with the absence of males, the largest most aggressive females shift sex to male. Dustin would never forget the time when he was twelve and his dad had helped him struggle to pull in a fifteen pounder. Although the mottled-gray fish could provide flaky white meat that most found delicious, this prize became his personal piece of wall art that was now somewhere in the attic. Although not so often since his return home, Dustin and his dad still loved fishing together, and Shay was getting old enough to start teaching. Fishing was one act that took no conversation, just being and relaxing. And sometimes that was all that men like he and his dad needed to show their love and commitment to one another. Just be and relax together while dropping a hook in the water. Since Dustin had served in the military and was a combat veteran, he now understood far better than before his father who was a Vietnam War veteran. His mom had remained dedicated to the family and was a positive spirit, although Dustin knew she had experienced some difficult times and numerous worries as the wife and mom of military men that had served in combat.

His mom and dad had met after his dad returned to Panama City Beach from two tours in Vietnam and separating from the Marine Corps. Following the Corps, he worked as a welder at the ship yard in Panama City back across Hathaway Bridge. It was 1974 and they were both with friends listening to live music by a local band called The Swingin' Medallions at The Hangout. The venue was popular with everyone that loved music, dancing, and holding out hope to meet someone special. The white building trimmed in bright red stood for decades on the beach until hurricane Eloise swept it away in 1975. After his dad spotted the tanned black haired cutie with the infectious laugh, and light hearted humor, his heart was snatched from him like a flower in a wind gust.

Maxie had smiled back at the tall handsome former Marine after catching his gaze and the enticing grin pasted across his face. When he walked to her and requested a dance to *I Found A Rainbow* that the band was performing, Maxie accepted. By the end of several more dances and exchanges of laughter, she also lost her heart. They dated from that night on and married in 1976. Shiloh was born in 1979 and Dustin in 1982. No doubt, his mom had her hands full.

Dustin reigned in his thoughts and laid down the newspaper. He walked to the rescue vehicle and validated that all the medical equipment and supplies were in order. After the job was completed, while shooting the breeze with other crew members, he heard the voice of his favorite person.

"Hey, Daddy, we brought you some lunch."

When Dustin turned, Shay and Maxie were walking toward him. Shay carried a plastic dish with food for his dad.

"Hi Buddy. Thanks. I'm starving. You're just in time! I might not have made it another minute!"

Shay laughed. "Oh Dad. You're being silly." Then he handed the dish to Dustin.

Dustin turned and hugged Maxie. "Mom, thanks. But I've told you that you don't have to do this."

"Well I know that. But I've told you that since I couldn't provide good meals for you when you were away in the military and deployed to those deserts and mountains, I'm darn well going to do it now. That is until you find the right woman to do it for you."

"Mom, I don't even know if women like to cook as much anymore. That's why you taught me to cook, remember? So I could take care of myself just in case cooking by wives went out of style?"

"Well, I'm not your wife. I'm your mother. Just let me enjoy it. And by the way, I went to the dentist this morning to get my teeth cleaned. There's a pretty new girl there who recently moved here. And I didn't see any engagement or wedding rings. You might should make yourself a dental appointment and ask for the hygienist named Kerra."

Dustin controlled his mild aggravation. "Mom, you gotta stop it! I keep telling you my life is full. I don't think I can fit anyone else in. And besides, I have too many flaws for anyone but a loving mother to put up with. You know better than anyone that combat vets have a few issues that most women don't want to deal with. No need in causing anyone else aggravation or setting myself up to fail."

"Oh, hogwash! You say that only because you haven't met the one that makes your blood rush and your eyes light up like when your dad and I met."

"Hey, Mom, too much information."

Maxie kept on. "Your dad wasn't the easiest to live with after Vietnam. But I loved him enough to learn patience. I also learned to kick him in the shin when he was too stubborn to get the help he needed just like I've done with you."

"Mom, I appreciate all your wisdom, but..."

Maxie, stood with her hands on her hips and interrupted her son.

"Well, just remember, you deserve being loved by a good woman. And Shay deserves not only a Gammie but a good mom, too."

Just as Maxie was about to say something else, an emergency call came in.

"Sorry Mom, gotta leave for this call. I'll see you guys in the morning."

Dustin gave Shay a quick kiss on top of his blonde head and turned toward the rescue truck. Someone was caught in a rip current.

Dustin and his partner, Jason Chase, quickly entered the vehicle and turned on the siren to travel east on Front Beach Road. The fire truck followed behind. As he drove, Dustin kept his calm to navigate as locals and tourists in vehicles found places to pull over and make way for the emergency sirens. He focused with this job as he did on the dangerous roads in the war zones where avoiding suspicious looking vehicles with bombs or places on roads where improvised explosive devices were buried was the difference between living and dying. One mistake while pressing to reach someone in danger or injured could shift an outcome that no one wanted to face.

Sirens continued as the fire truck driver blasted his horn. The traffic in front of the emergency vehicles continued shifting to the left and right to halt on the sandy shoulders of the two lane road.

"Rescue Station One, how far are you from adult and child caught in rip current at public access 56?"

"Two minutes," replied Jason.

"10-4."

Seconds later, Dustin caught site of a car coming from a side street headed toward the passenger door of the rescue vehicle. He laid down on his horn, and with precision he whipped wide around the front of the car. The car tires squealed to a stop just as the fire truck passed.

Dustin turned at the next immediate right and drove over the beach sand as near as possible to the gulf waters. On lookers watched an adult male who fought to reach a child. Although a lifeguard was in the water and paddling to the situation, Dustin threw off his uniform shirt, shoes and socks and grabbed the surf board from the top of his vehicle. With a life preserver in tow he raced into the water. With one powerful jump he landed on top of the board and paddled with all the strength his well trained muscles provided. Even in the water's heavy current Dustin moved swiftly. In moments he reached the man who struggled to keep the young girl from sinking. Dustin tossed the life preserver to him, and placed his hands gently on the thrashing, screaming child. Just as he thought she was secure, the girl broke from his grip and slipped beneath the water. Dustin tore the leash of the surf board from his ankle and dove into the current that was carrying the child downward.

"I'm not going to lose you," was his only thought.

With the kick of the Olympian he could have been, he reached the girl and grabbed her around her small waist. He rose to the top of the water with her against his chest.

Jason paddled quickly to Dustin where he took the girl, placed her on his surf board and paddled as quickly as his arms would let him back toward the beach. Dustin grabbed his board that somehow had managed not to be swept away. He easily passed Jason, threw his board down on the beach edge and raced back into the water. He took the girl from Jason and ran with her back to the beach sand where he performed CPR.

After a moment, she choked and spit out salt water. Then she cried. Dustin spoke gently.

"Hey, you're okay. What a trooper you are. Your mom and dad are right here. They're going to be with you for a little trip with these friends."

The medic with gloves and stethoscope checked the youngster's heart and breathing before she was placed in the ambulance taking her for a full evaluation at the hospital across the bridge in Panama City.

The crowd applauded, shouted and whistled for Dustin and other team members for the great job they had executed.

Dustin shook Jason's hand. "Hey man, good work. Thanks."

Afterwards, he walked away to be alone for a few moments to bring his breathing and adrenaline rush under control. Dustin had learned a method years before that his coach had taught him for fighting anxiety before swim meets.

"It only takes your body three minutes to react to adrenaline and three minutes to regain control," the coach told him. "So, if you focus on calming yourself down by counting to 10 in a controlled manner, you'll give your mind a message to relax."

It seemed that for all the hundreds, maybe thousands of times that Dustin had remembered to do this on the battlefield and during his transition off the battlefield, that he'd be rid of adrenalin rushes for the rest of his life. But today proved, once more, that the body always knows best and that "adrenalin does a body good." He also needed to take a moment to close his eyes and say a word of thanks that one more life under his responsibility had been spared. He wasn't a religious man. And life as a combat medic had left him with more questions than answers. But he believed in saying thank you to whatever power existed to help bring good.

Back at the station and in dry clothing, Dustin swiftly ate the meatloaf and potatoes his mom and Shay had brought earlier. He swallowed the food with too few chews as though someone was going to take it away from him. A habit created while he was in the military and couldn't seem to break. His mom always commented with: "Son, no well mannered woman is going to want to eat with a man that eats so fast and furious he's an embarrassment to be seen out with."

"You married Dad, didn't you?" Dustin always replied between gulps.

"Only because I never saw him eat in public and we couldn't afford to dine out."

It seemed his mom always had the last word.

On Friday evening at the dental office, Sarah locked the front door as Kerra straightened magazines on tables in the waiting room.

"Hey, some girls are going with me to a club for little black dress night. Wanna come with us?"

Kerra looked up from the magazines and smiled.

"Mmmm, sounds like fun. But I'm not sure about going tonight. Can I take a rain check?"

"Sure. We get together once a month on a Friday night."

"Okay. Remind me next month. I'll be a bit more acclimated to the job and maybe feeling like some night life by then."

"You got it. I'm holding you to it."

Closed for the weekend, everyone exited the back door of the dental office and went to their various vehicles to go home, the grocery store, day care, or wherever their personal lives led them on a Friday evening. Kerra was happy with her first week on the new job. Sarah was the youngest of the staff and single. The other two hygienists, Vicki and Lois, were both married with children, and Mrs. Dunson, the widowed office manager, had worked for Dr. Smith for years before he expanded the business to include Dr. Young.

Although she had driven her car from Wisconsin, Kerra lived close enough to her job to walk to and from work in nice weather. She felt safe since the half mile walk took her past both the police and Fire & Rescue Station. In the mornings and evenings she often saw some of the guys running together or washing trucks and equipment.

She waved and smiled at them and they reciprocated. They had tough jobs this time of year to keep up with accidents and potential tragedies like the one she had read about in the local newspaper last Tuesday morning. She had been impressed when she read about the rescue team member that had been asked what he thought about being called a hero for helping save a father and daughter from a rip current. He seemed very humble and modest when he said, "We're not heroes. We're just people who never know how far we can go until we're in situations that call for all we can possibly do to make a positive difference."

Kerra had wondered the rest of the week which one of the crew members from Fire and Rescue Station One had made the statement. Had she seen him running or received a reciprocating wave from him? That was the type of man Kerra wanted to speak to, shake his hand, and thank him for his public service.

Kerra stopped at the cross-walk and waited for the traffic light to change. While waiting, she checked her cell phone and tapped a number.

"Hi Mom, it's me. Give me a call when you get this. Nothing's wrong. Just checking in."

Summer weekend traffic jammed both sides of Front Beach Road. After the light changed, Kerra jogged across the street and down the path to the cottage. She inserted the key into the lock. Before she pushed the door open, she heard a noise and stopped to listen. There it was again, the sound of a young kitten. Kerra stepped back down the steps of the cottage deck. She looked to the right toward the palm tree and flower bed.

"Well, hello little one. Where'd you come from?" The kitten looked up with another weak meow. "Are you going to let me pick you up or run?" Kerra reached toward the handful of black fur with white boots. It backed up with a hiss. "Okay, she said. Don't go anywhere. I'll get some milk for you."

Thirty minutes later Kerra sat perched on the beach with her chair, magazines, and the umbrella secured well into the sand. She flipped through the pages of *Woman's World* and stopped at the article, "Funny Secret to Making More Friends!" Before she completed the piece, she answered her phone and began a report before her mom could speak.

"Hello! I had a great first week on the new job. Co-workers are wonderful. I've met some wonderful people. I've enjoyed walking to and from work, watching beautiful sunrises and sunsets, and right now I'm sitting at the beach catching up on new information in my magazine."

"Well that sounds like a great way to end a work week. I'm jealous."

"I know you are! Hey! Here's something. You're always concerned about my ability to make new and more friends. Well, listen to this. A new study in the journal *Personality and Individual Differences* says that people will connect to others and look forward to spending more time with them after making a joke or pointing out something funny. I guess I need to find a joke book and learn some conversation starters."

"That's pretty informative, honey. Maybe I should add that to my to do list."

"Oh mom, you're already full of personality."

"Don't flatter me so! By the way, you sound happy."

"I really am, Mom. This is a beautiful place even if traffic is bumper to bumper. Being near the water and hearing the music of the seagulls and surf is therapeutic, especially early mornings and in the evenings."

"We miss you, but you know that all your family wants for you is happiness." Sylvia's tone seemed to change.

"I know Mom. Hey, now you're sounding kind of melancholy. Is everything okay?"

"Sweetie, we received a phone call today. Winston is back in the hospital."

Kerra became quiet. "Are you there, honey?"

"Yes Mom. I'm here. I just feel awful that Winston, for all his life's goodness, the brother I never had, is suffering so. And I get to be here enjoying this beautiful beach and beginning a new life. I feel so guilty. I should have never left."

"Kerra, please don't do this to yourself. There is nothing you could do even if you were here."

"It doesn't feel that way, Mom. I wonder over and over if I abandoned Winston by leaving Augusta. I wonder if there has ever been anything else I could do to help him have a better life since the accident. We were always so close. We were best friends from the time we were babies."

"Honey, just pray for peace and healing. It can help lift the burden you carry and the issues that Winston is working hard to get through."

"I know you're right, Mom. You're so right. But it's difficult to 'let go and let God,' when we don't even understand why bad things happen to good people. But thanks for reminding me."

"I promise we will all continue to help Winston and his parents. This is a small town here, you know that. We do all we can to take care of our own."

"Thanks, Mom. I love you much. Give Dad a hug for me. Tell him I love him. And the same to Sis one and three when you talk to them."

"I will, Sweetheart. Enjoy the sunset and sleep well tonight."

"Sure thing."

Kerra pressed the End Call button and returned the cell phone to her bag. She leaned her head against the back of her chair, sighed and watched the sun dressed in a blaze of orange ease behind the horizon while she whispered a prayer.

CHAPTER THREE

On Saturday morning Maxie poured pancake mix into a bowl, added water and began whipping. There was once a time when she would only make pancakes from scratch, but she had finally accepted the fact that Hungry Jack made the process much easier and faster. She hummed a tune from years ago, "The Happiest Girl in the Whole USA" by mostly forgotten country singer, Donna Fargo.

With the batter well mixed, Maxie clanged baking sheets together as she pulled the one she wanted from the drawer beneath the stove. She lined the pan with aluminum foil and placed strips of bacon to oven fry. This was the weekend breakfast special for her husband, Hugh. And always ready by 7:00 a.m. For all the years that he had worked at the ship yard, often seven days a week, and provided for their family, hearty meals made by her hands was his favorite thing. Now, after forty years and movement into management, he no longer worked on Saturdays unless called for an emergency.

"Good morning, beautiful. How's my girl?"

"Well, now. You sound pretty chipper this morning. Something going on I don't know about?"

"Maybe it's from all that cuddlin' last night."

"Oh, shut up," Maxie said, while stirring the pancake batter again and hiding a sly smile.

Her husband placed his hands on her shoulders and kissed the top of her head. He had shown Maxie affection in this way for the many years they had shared. Years that carried downs as well as many wonderful ups. He just always hoped that if one day he had to review a chalkboard in the great beyond, that the ups would have a greater number listed than the downs he was responsible for. He slid to the right of Maxie and removed a coffee mug from the cabinet with no doors.

"I do have a surprise for you today."

"Oh really, Mr. Brites." Maxie slid the spatula beneath a pancake and flipped it in the skillet.

"Our son and I are going to put the refinished doors back on your cabinets today."

Dustin and his dad had started the kitchen remodel four months ago. The new ceramic floor tile, new plumbing, back splash and counter tops were complete. A wall was removed so Maxie could enjoy her HGTV dream of a large open space for cooking, dining, and living.

Maxie turned with a squeal and almost knocked the cup of coffee from Hugh's hand. "You're kiddin' me?"

"No, Mom. No kiddin'." Dustin walked in from his twenty-four hour shift. "By this evening you'll have your dishes behind closed doors."

"Oh, "Behind Closed Doors." Hugh began singing the song made famous by Charlie Rich in 1973. He sat the cup of coffee on the counter, pulled his wife close and began a slow dance.

"Uh, I'd advise you both to bring your attention back to the task at hand. Or there'll be no need for kitchen cabinets."

"Take care of that. Will you son? We're busy."

Dustin had already grabbed a kitchen towel and lifted the smoking skillet with the burned pancake from the stove.

"What's going on? It's noisy in here."

Shay was standing with sleep filled eyes and wearing dolphin covered pajamas made by Maxie.

"Hey Buddy, it's just your grandparents acting a little silly this morning. Sorry we disturbed your sleep."

Dustin picked up his four year old and gave him a tight hug and a kiss on the side of his face. "You ready to help Pops and me work on Gammies's kitchen today?"

"Actually," said Maxie as she pushed away from Hugh and placed her attention back on preparing breakfast, "I promised Shay a trip to the zoo this morning to see the new baby lemur exhibit. For ten dollars he can have a lemur encounter."

Shay's eyes widened with excitement.

"Dad, that means I can go inside the lemur house and play with them. How cool is that?" Dustin put Shay down so they could take a seat for breakfast. Shay kicked his legs beneath the table while waiting on Maxie for pancakes and bacon.

"That's about the coolest thing I've heard lately." Dustin said. "I've never done that before. You promise to tell me all about it when you get back home?"

"Yes sir. I will." Shay switched focus to working with his fork to get a slice of pancake into his mouth. Dustin looked at his son, smiled and scrubbed his knuckles gently across the top of the boy's head.

Kerra placed more milk in the bowl outside by the palm tree in case the kitten returned, then began her brisk walk down the beach. She smiled and said hello to those who looked in her direction. She felt the growing strength of her legs and calf muscles since her beach walks began more than a month ago. The early peaceful mornings with the gentle spill of the surf against the shore of white sand had the ability to bring a hurting soul some peace. A few others strolled and jogged along the shore for exercise and meditative thoughts. By 10:00 a.m. the sand would be consumed by beach goers out for tans and fun with friends, family, children or lovers.

Seagulls floated on air overhead and pelicans rested on the water near shore. The sky was clear blue, although the weather channel called for afternoon showers, which Kerra had learned could blow in at a moment's notice and disappear as quickly. The heat and humidity would rise by the hour. A lone fisherman leaned against a railing at the end of the pier and waited on a strike against his fishing line. Kerra sipped from her water bottle. She decided to take the steps to the top of the pier and pay the two dollar fee to walk its length and see a view of the coastline not available by walking along the shore. She looked over the railings to see if any stingrays were visible. They were known to live in temperate coastal waters, mostly inactive and partially buried in the sand. This morning she smiled with pleasure as a few of them swayed in a gentle dance with the tide. After the stingrays moved from sight, Kerra continued strolling down the pier to the end. She watched the fisherman reel in his line holding only an empty hook.

"Darn it," he snapped. He looked to be around Kerra's age, had a handsome face, was average height, and had a good build as though he worked out. As he turned to replace the bait on his hook, he spotted her.

"Hi there. Sorry 'bout that. It's aggravating when dolphins keep stealing my dinner off the line."

Kerra looked from side to side beyond the pier railings until she finally spotted several dolphins arcing and disappearing with grace and ease in the emerald waters.

"That is so beautiful!" She said while searching to see where fins might pop up next.

The man worked at putting more bait on the line.

"They're beautiful, graceful and often a great help against sharks, but they are pests for fisherman. I think that smile on their face is just their way of saying, 'Hey, got you on that one!'"

"That's pretty funny. I see you have a sense of humor." Kerra laughed and searched again for dolphins.

"You from here or a visitor?" The man asked as he continued fiddling with the fish hook.

"One or the other," Kerra said. She didn't want to share information with a stranger.

"Oh, a bit sarcastic are we? Well, I'm Jason. Excuse me if I don't shake your hand but its fishy smelling at the moment."

"No problem. And sorry if I sound sarcastic, it's just that a girl can't be too careful, you know. I'm Kerra."

"You like to fish?"

"Can't say I like it. I've only tried it a few times in a lake with a cane pole."

Kerra noticed others arriving on the pier pulling their carts holding various fishing apparatus, coolers, outdoor chairs and umbrellas for protection from the sun or potential rain.

"You wanna give salt water fishing a try?" Jason raised his eye brows with the question and also presented a sexy grin.

"I'd probably catch the hook on someone. It's getting crowded out here."

"Nah. You'll do fine." Jason held the fishing rod toward Kerra. "Here, take it. If you're not afraid I'll bite, I'll show you how to cast it. I just need you to stand here in front of me."

Kerra felt safe with others now gathered around them. If he tried anything she could scream. Once in place and holding up the fishing rod with her right hand, Jason placed his hand over hers.

"Okay, we're going to bring the rod back easy to the right of your shoulder." He helped her with the motion. "Now, cast it forward while letting go of the spindle."

Again, Jason helped her with the motion, his hand still on hers. Kerra watched the line make its way out and across the water and heard the plop of the lure into the depth.

"Now," he said, "wind the reel a bit until the slack comes out and the line tightens."

Kerra concentrated as Jason had her reel in the line and re-cast. By the fourth try, Kerra was giggling. "I think I've got this!"

"Yep, you just might have potential."

Kerra handed the fishing rod back to Jason with a relaxed smile. "Thanks, that was fun. And actually something I'd never thought to put on my bucket list."

"My pleasure, Miss Kerra." Jason paused a moment to fiddle again with bait. "But aren't you kind of young for a bucket list?"

"Oh…I don't think so. Some life experiences have taught me that no one is ever too young for a bucket list." Watching Jason, Kerra became curious. "Are you a local or a tourist?"

"Oh, I'm a home boy. Came here when I was about thirteen. My dad retired from Tyndall Air Force base about 40 miles up the road to the east. With all the different places we lived before coming here, I never wanted to move any place else. Went to college in Tallahassee. Then came home and got lucky enough to join Fire and Rescue Station One here on the beach."

Kerra was suddenly interested. She leaned the small of her back against the pier railing while Jason leaned forward and relaxed with his fishing line in the water.

"I read the news article about the heroic rescue you guys made last week," she said.

"Nothing heroic about it," Jason said. And reeled in another empty fish hook. "We just try to do the job we're hired for."

Something about that comment sounded familiar to Kerra.

"Well, you and your team did a great thing in saving that dad and his little girl. Don't underestimate what you do for your community, even if you are paid for it."

"Thanks. That's nice of you to say. Believe it or not, the local fire and rescue was mostly volunteers until the early 90's. And paid or not, the difficult part of the job is always about those we can't reach in time."

"I would imagine that has to be very difficult. I've had a different situation to deal with, but I kind of understand what you're saying. Anyway, thanks again for a new adventure this morning. I've got to go and finish my exercise and run some errands before beach traffic gets out of control."

Jason reeled in his line and leaned the rod against the pier rail. "Before you leave, could I ask you a question?"

"Sure."

"Are you busy later this evening?"

"No, not really." Kerra shifted her weight from one foot to another and pulled at her pony tail.

"I'd like to invite you to dinner and some music, if that's okay."

Kerra hesitated a moment before responding. "Sure. That sounds like fun. Is there a particular place we can meet?"

"Isn't it customary for a guy to pick up the girl for a date?"

"Well, I don't want you to pick me up, I might be too heavy." Kerra grinned.

Jason finally concentrated on her more than attractive face and perfect teeth. "Well, you got me didn't you. I see you have your own jokes."

"Well, yes, it's a joke. But since I'm so new in town, I'm just cautious."

"So, you do live around here," Jason said.

"Yes, I moved here in May. And I hope you won't mind if I meet you at a location."

"That's fine. How about 8:00 p.m. at Harpoon Harry's on Front Beach Road. Great food and good music. You familiar with it?"

"I can find it," said Kerra. "See you there."

Jason watched as she jogged back toward the pier's entrance. "I think I got the best catch of the day," he thought with a tremendous smile. Then he packed away his fishing gear and headed out to help Dustin work on the remodel project at Mr. and Mrs. Brites' home. He couldn't wait to tell Dustin about Kerra.

CHAPTER FOUR

Kerra drove her Volkswagen Bug down Front Beach Road and turned right into the parking lot of the restaurant. She was fortunate that someone was backing out from a parking space as she made the second round in her search to park. She and Jason had agreed to meet at 8:00 p.m. It was 7:55. The restaurant looked like two different buildings connected by an adjoining wall. The side to the left was weathered gray clap board with whimsical tiki torches and Hawaiian party décor. She could see all the way through the front entrance to the tiki bar tables with lime green umbrellas, then the beach. Live music drifted from the patio. The right side appeared more formal with tall glass double doors. This is where Jason told her to enter and meet him.

As Kerra opened the door, she spotted Jason talking and laughing with the hostess. He was dressed in kaki Dockers shorts, a black t-shirt with the words "Salt Life" on the back, and boat shoes. His clean cut light brown hair had a shine, appearing still damp.

"Hey, fisherman, you clean up pretty well."

Jason turned from the hostess toward Kerra. "Hey there," he said with an irresistible smile. "I didn't know if you'd show or if you were just trying to *cast* me off this morning."

"*Cast* you off. Are you trying to be funny again with a play on words?"

"Maybe."

" Well, I have better manners than that," Kerra grinned. "I would have told you up front if I didn't want to meet for dinner."

The hostess and another girl wrote down names and party numbers for others lining up for dinner. A sign read *Lobster Special $29.95.*

"You ready, Jason." Another hostess appeared.

"Sure thing. I'm starving and I'm sure my new friend Kerra is, too."

The tall hostess was pleasant. "Hi Kerra. Nice to meet you. Just look out for this guy, he's the local heartbreaker."

"Oh really!" Kerra lifted her eyebrows. "Well it's a good thing I'm not in the market to give my heart away! No give, no break!"

"Now Kim, there you go again exaggerating, trying to mess things up for me," Jason said jokingly as he and Kerra followed the hostess to the dining table.

Kim laughed and pulled out the two chairs at the table covered by a white cloth with a candle glowing in the center.

"I'm just teasing, Kerra. Jason's a good guy. We all know him and the crew from Rescue Station One. We just love giving the few single guys a hard time when they come in. Enjoy your evening. A waiter will be right with you."

Kerra ordered water with lemon and Jason ordered a glass of wine. Both ordered the lobster special with salads.

"So, what did you do with the rest of your day?" Jason asked as he sipped from the glass of water that had already been provided.

"I ran some errands, and then I stopped by the zoo. I didn't even know Panama City Beach had a zoo until I passed it on my way to another location."

"It's a nice place to spend a few hours. Did they have any new exhibits?"

"My favorite was the baby lemurs. I watched a little boy having the best time. He laughed and giggled while the furry critters set on his head, shoulders, and jumped from one place to the other."

"So, you like kids?"

"I do. I have two nephews back home."

"And where is back home?"

"Augusta, Wisconsin, about 230 miles from Milwaukee," Kerra said, as she smiled at the waiter who placed dinner plates in front of her and Jason.

"Wow! An entire lobster!" She picked up hers by the claws and with the tail on her plate, did a little puppet dance.

"Do you always play with your food when you go out?" Jason laughed.

"Only when I'm out with a guy and I want to see if he runs off when I act silly."

"Not me. Gotta laugh."

"And what brought you here to our great little beach community? Jason asked.

"You know it gets pretty cold in Wisconsin in winter. I decided I wanted a change, so here I am."

"I guess trading sugar white snow for our sugar sand beaches isn't a bad deal. I know I couldn't live in snow. My dad was stationed in Colorado once. I learned to snow board there when I was a kid. But I like beach living much better."

"Can't blame you there," Kerra said in total agreement. "I grew up in snow and sub zero winters. Makes me cold just thinking about it."

"So, Miss Kerra, you know what I do for a living. May I ask what you do? Or are you independently wealthy and just enjoy each day as you like it?"

"Sure. In my dreams." Kerra took a sip of water. "I'm a dental hygienist at Smith and Young's not far from the Rescue Station."

"No kiddin'. I think just about all the crew goes there for their dental work."

"Well that means I might get to dig around in your mouth next time you come in for a cleaning. So, be nice. It could be the difference between gentleness and pain." Kerra made a motion with the fork she held in her hand

"I actually think I'd like that. I'll make sure to ask for you! And by the way, have I told you how nice you look this evening?" Jason leaned back in his chair and straightened his back. He placed the tips of his fingers on the edge of the table.

Kerra was wearing denim shorts with a white sleeveless top and scooped neck. Her dangling silver earrings matched the silver choker with a turquoise stone in the center. Her auburn hair was pulled away from her face into the ponytail she liked to wear. And she wore minimal makeup.

"Would you like a glass of wine or some desert?"

"No, I'm good. And thank you for the compliment." Kerra provided a courteous smile and then picked up her purse from the floor beside her right foot. Jason noticed that she was pulling money from her wallet.

"And what are you doing?" asked Jason.

"I'm going to pay for my dinner."

"Oh, no you're not. I asked you out this evening. It's my treat."

Kerra didn't want to make this a real date situation. But she didn't want to offend Jason.

"Okay, this time," she said. "But if there's a next time it's on me."

"Man, you are one independent woman, aren't you?"

"Well, dinners cost a lot. It's a rough economy right now." Kerra shrugged her shoulders and leaned her head sort of sideways.

After Jason paid the bill, he led Kerra to the outdoor patio for the live music and where others were dancing. When the musician began to play a slow song, Jason asked Kerra to dance.

"Sure, I'll try but I might step on your feet."

"No problem. I walk on the bottom, so you can walk on the top."

"Funny guy, you are." Kerra grinned and accepted Jason's hand to lead her to the dance area.

After the dance ended, Kerra wasn't sure how to feel about how tight Jason pressed his body against hers. She wasn't comfortable in feeling someone's belt buckle digging into her stomach.

"So, would you like to go for a walk on the beach?" Jason asked as he held Kerra's hands in his.

"Can I take a rain check?" Kerra asked. "Actually I'm a bit tired. I've been up since early this morning. And I have a new kitten I need to check on."

"But it's only ten o'clock. The party hasn't even started!"

"I know. I'll plan better next time. Get a nap in before I go out."

"Okay, if you insist. I'll walk you to your car."

After they reached the Volkswagen and Kerra unlocked her door, Jason leaned toward her. Kerra turned her face before he could kiss her on the lips. As she sat down in her car seat, Jason placed his hands in his pockets. "Hey, I really enjoyed your company. Hope we can do it again. You drive careful."

"I will. You do the same. See you later," Kerra said politely, then pulled the car door closed and started the engine. Jason walked back toward the music as Kerra found her way back to Front Beach Road and toward the cottage.

CHAPTER FIVE

The chance of rain for Saturday made its appearance early Sunday morning. Gentle and easy was what the grass and plants needed. The tap on the roof kept Kerra snuggled beneath the comforter. That is until her cell phone buzzed. She picked up the phone knowing it was either her mom or one of her sisters.

"Mornin' Mom." Kerra yawned and shifted the bed covers.

"Good morning! You don't sound like you're up and at 'em yet. Are you still in bed?"

"Well yes, I am. Was up later than usual watching television and reading." Kerra didn't dare tell her mom she had gone out with Jason and give her fodder for bugging her.

"And by the way mom, I'm not a kid at the farm anymore. I don't have to get up early to help milk the cows."

Sylvia laughed. "You're right. Your time is yours now. Sorry I woke you. But you know I'm going to worry until I get used to you being away from here. And what if I never get used to that?"

Kerra threw the covers back and swung her legs from the bed. "Mom, I love you for loving me and your other kids so much. I promise I'll call later and we'll catch up."

"Alright. I love you."

"Love you, too, Mom. Later."

Kerra hit the End Call button before her mom had another chance to speak.

By noon, the rain and dark clouds had blown away to uncover the blue sky. Kerra sipped a cup of tea as she walked outside to see if the kitten was around. She sat down in the Adirondack chair beneath the palm tree. Hoping the kitten would become friendlier through a little play time, Kerra picked up the small rope with a little mouse and a bell on the end and swung it gently. She couldn't tell where the kitten came from, but it eased up and sat down a few feet from her and moved its head back and forth watching the mouse's movement.

"Hey, little one," Kerra whispered. "It looks like you're getting fatter."

The kitten moved from its haunches and with a playful paw struck at the swinging mouse.

"There you go." Kerra smiled. "I think we could be friends. Don't you? We could be good company for one another right here in our own little piece of paradise."

Just as Kerra reached her hand towards the kitten, a siren sounded and the kitten barreled away. Kerra followed its movement to beneath a bush near the back side of the cottage where the screened patio was located. "Hah! Well, now I know where you hide," she said to herself. "We'll play again later, okay. I think I need something to eat."

Another hunger pang struck inside Kerra's stomach. She opened the refrigerator and took out the fresh baby spinach, shallots, and baby bella mushrooms she purchased at the grocery store the day before. She discovered the recipe for the antioxidant rich Lemony Sauteed Spinach and Mushrooms in the most current issue of *Woman's World.* As called for by the recipe she heated 1 tablespoon of olive oil in a skillet, then stirred eight ounces of mushrooms, a large shallot, and salt and pepper until they were browned. Next she added one-fourth cup of white wine and stirred until it evaporated. Kerra placed the mixture on a bright colored plate that came from among other colorful dishes in the kitchen cabinet. Then she cooked ten ounces of baby spinach on medium low until it wilted and then added to the mushroom mixture.

"Mmmmm," she said to herself and smiling. "Beautiful and healthy!"

With a glass of unsweetened black tea with lemon and ice in one hand and her plate in the other, Kerra walked to the table on the screened patio. She sat down, closed her eyes for a moment, then took a bite of the new recipe and savored life, if only for just a few seconds without feeling guilty.

The rear end collision that morning on Sail Street had not been life threatening to anyone. Just young drivers not paying attention. They were probably going to be hurt more by their parents than the collision itself. Dustin and Jason drove back to the station glad there was no more to it than bent bumpers and embarrassed teen drivers.

"So, how was your date last night?" Dustin asked as he repositioned the rear view mirror.

"Had a great time. But I think she's one of those wanting to play hard to get." Jason straightened his sunglasses.

"What makes you say that? Something to do with you couldn't get her to hit the sack with you on a first date? Losing your smooth, Mr. Smooth?" Dustin laughed and shook his head.

"Hey, man. I'm not worried. I'll see her again. She'll come around. They all do. Eventually."

"Yep, and then you let them down with some kind of story that breaks their heart. When you going to grow up, man?" Dustin turned the vehicle into the station and shut off the engine.

"Well, this might be the one," Jason replied in a serious tone. "This girl really has something different going on."

"Well, if that's the case, I wish you luck. Maybe another fishing lesson might help."

"Thanks, Dus. You know, you should think about meeting a good woman for yourself. That boy of yours could use a good mom."

"You're not the only one telling me that. It's just not the right time. I've still got baggage and issues to get cleared before I risk bringing someone else into my life."

The two men exited the truck and headed toward the kitchen to get something to eat from the refrigerator.

"Hey, you two! What took so long?" The rest of the Sunday crew was already seated hoping a call wouldn't come in. Maxie had placed an entire meal on the long wooden table for everyone. Shay was helping by giving everyone a plastic cup for tea.

"Here's some baked chicken, green salad, green beans and bread. I know you all like to watch your waistlines, but I made a cheesecake too."

"Mrs. Brites, you are one in a million!" Jason walked toward the woman he considered a second mom and gave her a big hug.

"Thanks, Mom. You know the guys really appreciate this." There was no use trying to talk her out of cooking a complete meal once a month for the team. She loved playing mom to as many as possible, and she would have it no other way.

"I had to bring my boys a good meal. After all, most of you helped get my new kitchen completed, up and running yesterday. I had to bring you one of the first meals cooked on my new stove!"

"Okay boys, we better eat before that next call comes in." Dustin gave his mom and Shay a hug and then a kiss on the sides of their faces.

"Dad?" Shay asked. "Can I tell a joke before me and Gammie go?"

"Well sure Buddy. We would love that."

"Okay, this is a question joke," Shay said with all eyes on him.

"Why do sharks live in saltwater?"

"We don't know!" the crew shouted in unison. "Why do sharks live in saltwater?"

"Because pepper makes them sneeze!" Shay laughed and slapped his small hands on his thighs. "That's a good one isn't it?"

"You bet it is." Everyone laughed in response to the youngster as he walked by each crew member and issued a high five.

After Maxie and Shay left, Dustin sat down with his team. As food bowls passed around the table from one to another, they all laughed at a joke Jason came up with. Dustin laughed, too. Then he contemplated for a moment about folks saying he needed a good woman. He had a job, co-workers, and family he loved dearly, and he was loved. Why would he need more? He had experienced the best and worst of life by the time he was twenty-six years old. He didn't set his sights or hopes on anything more or less than living a moment at a time. Since 9/11, he had come to a full understanding that anything could change in the blink of an eye. He had come to view the world, life, and living in a manner that only those like him understood. With the potential to earn an Olympic title in a swimming pool, he had selected a different path as a young man of twenty after seeing on television the fall of the twin towers in New York on 9/11/2001, the death toll after the terrorists flew flight number 77 into the Pentagon, and the courage of American civilians that overtook another flight from terrorists and brought the plane to crash into a Pennsylvania corn field instead of the White House.

Yes, this had been the day of infamy that Dustin would never forget, just as the day of infamy at Pearl Harbor that his grandfather Claude, his father's father, always spoke of with clarity until his death at age ninety-one.

Dustin remembered when his grandpa learned about his intention to enlist in the Army. Claude asked him to visit his bedside at the area Veteran's home. Although his body was fully broken, and he had accepted the embarrassment of nurses changing his diapers and giving him baths, his mind had not lost a beat with time.

"Son," he said after Dustin arrived that day. "War is no good. It's ugly. There's nothing heroic about it. It's about surviving and helping protect the men you grow to love that are in the trenches with you. Don't have any misconceptions. You'll leave here an innocent boy, but you'll come back a scarred and different man. Maybe a broken and wounded man. Someone that won't even recognize himself. Someone that others, even your family won't recognize. Someone that will need more strength than you can imagine to return to even a part of the person you were before going to war. That is if you make it back. And if you don't, people of your country may call you a hero or a baby killer, but your mother will only know the tears of a broken woman who will never fully heal because her son sacrificed himself. It may be called a sacrifice for a good cause. But only the future can tell if that's the truth or not. I made it back boy. Your daddy made it back from Vietnam, only to be spit on and cursed by an ungrateful nation. You don't have to do this with the possibility of falling into dark holes that a lot of war veterans never return from. We know the truths. We did enough already for this family and country. You don't need to feel the obligation."

Fighting back tears, Dustin had held his grandpa's frail hand gently. His skin was so thin that the lines of blood vessels appeared dark and thick. No one would have ever known that the shadow of life beneath the sheet had gone to WWII a strapping six foot two, muscular and strong, one hundred ninety pound man. He had been drafted into the Army as a mechanic since that was his occupation and had owned his own business in civilian life. His dad before him had owned the black smith shop in the same location across the bridge from the beach in the small town of Callaway. After boot camp, Claude's unit was sent straight into the thick of things. Being a mechanic, his unit was at the back of the fighting to keep the vehicles in as good of shape as possible. But when the Germans rolled in, they made their way through the Americans to the point where the mechanics were fighting for their lives. Claude and others were captured there at *The Battle of the Bulge*. They were gathered like cows for the slaughter and marched for days and into the months without their boots, with no food or water. Only at dark did the Germans stop and take their prisoners into confiscated barns or fields for the night. Each man received a sip of water and a bite of hard bread. Starvation made the rats scampering inside a barn become food targets. During a daily march, when an American soldier reached down to retrieve a piece of grass to eat from the side of the road, a German guard shot him in the hand. Claude and hundreds of others lived this way for over a year until early one morning when he and his companions awoke to voices outside the barn where they were placed the night before. Listening until they could obtain clarity, the prisoners suddenly yelled as loud as they could, "It's the Americans! They're here for us! We're in here!" they shouted. "We're in here!"

Claude's wife, Sally, finally received a telegram that her husband was found and in a military hospital. He would be returning to Martin Army Hospital at Fort Benning, Georgia for treatment and recovery. When Sally, the five foot tall, one-hundred pound woman with two small boys, finally saw her husband, he was only a 120 pound shadow of his former self. In the months and some years to come, alcohol abuse became Claude's crutch while returning to his garage business and fathering two more children. Sally's days were difficult. God and her church were her only shelter. Then one day when the small woman had enough, she called the police. Claude was taken back to Martin Army Hospital. After a week he stole away and walked and hitched rides for the two hundred miles back to Callaway. Afterwards, he never drank another drop. Although he became a man of few words and part of his personality became cold and iron clad. Claude's children never invited school friends to visit their home because they didn't want to have to explain their dad's lack of words and warmth towards others. It was only after Dustin became Claude's first grandchild that he rose above the lack of tenderness he had shown his own children.

Dustin had continued to hold his grandfather's hand. With the other he stroked him across the top of his white hair that was still kept groomed in a military style called a flat top.

"You see, Son, why I wish you'd think this idea of yours through again."

"Yes, Grandpa. I do. But I can do no less for my family and country than what you and dad did. Both of you made it back. You both returned home and became good citizens and good dads. "

Dustin's dad entered the conversation. He had driven his son to visit with Claude that day.

"I guess that's all in who you ask," he had said. "And at what time it was said after we returned. I have my own war stories. Most I've never spoken of. And your mom didn't have an easy time with me after we got married. There are things that happened before you were a spark in my eye that I'm not proud of. It took special women like your grandma Sally and your mom to always stand by me and your grandpa. They had to have grit and forgiveness, because I know your grandpa and I never knew how to get the most important words to come from our mouths. Men are strange enough. Military men can be even stranger. Add battlefield time to the mix and that creates an entirely different kind of man to deal with. We always wanted to be good husbands and fathers, but what battlefield veterans bring back home with us, Dustin, can change how good or bad each day can be. It's an emotional roller coaster ride for everyone. I know your grandmother hid stuff from me and my siblings, and your mom did too to keep you and your sister from being affected as much as possible by the aftermath of my war. We all know you are of the age to make your own decision. Your grandpa and I just wanted you to know as much as we could tell you about our personal experiences before you make the final decision about signing that dotted line. We promised your mother we would have this conversation with you. But we will all stand behind you, no matter your decision."

A week after the visit with his grandpa and dad, Dustin went to the Army recruiter's office. He didn't want to wait any longer, afraid that everything Claude and his dad had said would cause him to change his mind. With the presence of his mother and father, Dustin made his commitment. His mother fought back the tears and stood strong for him as she had done many times to support his father after Vietnam. After Dustin took the oath to the Constitution, Maxie hugged him tightly and whispered, "I'm so proud of you." He and his dad shook hands with a tight grip in the manner of two strong men.

A month later, in March 2002, he was in boot camp at Fort Benning, Georgia, where his grandfather had been. With his skills he was assigned to a Cavalry Regiment, and moved on to Medic training. The next six years were one deployment after the other between Afghanistan and Iraq. He had seen more than he could have ever comprehended, even after hearing his grandpa's experiences. Both his grandpa and dad were right on. He was a changed man in various ways. The difficulty was how to separate the good from the bad. How to get the dreams to stop that he didn't want his mom to know about and how to keep her from watching him stare into nothingness. He had seen her pressing back tears. He knew she was seeing similar things that she had seen with his dad, only Dustin was the son she delivered from her womb. And Dustin knew he had to do everything possible to be the dad that Shay deserved. The joy and delight that entered his life two years before he separated from the Army.

Dustin and a former high school classmate that he and his folks had always admired had visited together while he was home on leave before another deployment back to Afghanistan. He had told her that just in case he didn't make it back, he'd like to know that he had left a part of himself for his family. He told her that if she became pregnant before his actual deployment date back to the battlefields, he would add her name as a co- beneficiary for a portion of his military life insurance along with his parents who would help care for the baby in the event of his death. There would be a trust, and the baby would receive benefits as the child of a fallen soldier. Dustin and Gloria were both twenty-three. She would graduate from the local college in May and had no qualms with what Dustin had suggested.

Dustin learned of the pregnancy two and a half months later. He wrote an e-mail home to his parents, explaining the situation. They were taken aback at first, but accepted why their son would have done such a thing. And God grant he was not taken from them, but if he were, a part of him would be left with them in the flesh.

Dustin arranged all the paper work and beneficiary information as promised to Gloria.

To the thankfulness of everyone, Dustin returned from the war zone deployment after deployment for the next two years. But the woman that had agreed to carry Dustin's child died in a car accident when Shay was only six months old. Dustin's parents took over caring for Shay and sharing visits with Shay's maternal grandparents. But in their grief, Gloria's parents eventually moved from town and the sight where their daughter's car had been hit by a drunk driver on Front Beach Road.

Six months after separating from the Army, Dustin decided that the Veterans Administration was not the answer to problems he brought back home from war. His claim was in with his medical records to learn what percentage disability he would receive for two bad knees, a bad back, and broken elbow, loss of hearing, rattled brain cells from rocket propelled grenades and 50 caliber machine guns, and Post Traumatic Syndrome Dysfunction known best as PTSD. But the waiting was backed up for more than a year. While he waited to see what small pension he might receive and to pull himself together enough to transition from military life back to civilian life, his thoughts returned to his roots as a swimmer. With the help and encouragement of his parents, Dustin chose to put everything he had into becoming as much of his former self as possible.

He finally threw all the pain and anxiety meds down the toilet that the doctors and psychiatrists at the Veterans Clinic had given him. He began swimming or kayaking every day. Even if the majority of macho men didn't think it was cool, he attended a yoga class at the college that was led by a former Navy Seal. He changed his diet for better health. Within weeks, he could tell a definite difference in how he felt both mentally and physically. Although, the part that didn't work was trying to hang with old school friends that had not experienced the taste of war. He often ached for the comradeship of his military buddies that understood they weren't kids anymore living in a charmed world of text messaging and cyber space. There was much evil to be feared in today's world. But only the less than one percent of America's population, the United States military, that had come face to face with such evil truly understood.

When the emergency alarm sounded Dustin's attention returned to the present. A car was on fire in the median on Back Beach Road. *"Toujours Pret,"* he whisperd. *"Always Ready. "*

CHAPTER SIX

As usual, Kerra arrived for work early on Monday morning. She liked plenty of time to review files on the day's patients and set up examination rooms. She noticed that Mrs. Brites was returning today for a follow up on a cavity by Doctor Smith. Sarah turned the office music to a low volume. By 8:50 a.m. all the staff arrived in the break room for a quick chat.

"Did anyone do anything extraordinarily fun or interesting this weekend?" Sarah was the first to lift her cheery voice. Being the youngest of the staff, she always had something to share about a new guy she had met or something crazy happening at Club La Vela. So sweet and innocent, Kerra always thought to herself.

Everyone else clung to their coffee or tea cups and found a thought or two about their kid's soccer practice or a bit of "did you see this or that from the Sunday newspaper." All that Kerra had to offer for the morning was a smile and that she was trying to tame the kitten that hung around the cottage. At 9:00 a.m. sharp Sarah unlocked the front door for patients. Maxie crossed the threshold first along with Shay. Just as they were settled in chairs with a book in Shay's hand, Maxie heard Kerra's voice calling her name.

"Good morning! Kerra from Wisconsin. Right?" Maxie said as she followed Kerra and took a seat in the dental chair.

"You remembered!" Kerra sat down on the stool next to Maxie and patted her on the arm.

"I'm getting some squeaks and leaks in me, but I'm not losing my memory. Yet, that is!"

Kerra laughed as she pulled on medical gloves and placed the clips on the dental napkin that lay on Maxie's chest. "Okay, open wide and let me see what my little mirror reflects for me up there?"

As Kerra returned the tool to the tray, Doctor Smith entered the exam room.

"Well good morning Miss Maxie. What are we doing this morning?"

"A cavity fill. Remember."

"You know Maxie, both of us have some age on us. I don't know about you but I have to have reminders now and then."

Maxie and Donald Smith had gone from grade school through high school together. After Donald completed college and dental school, he returned and opened his office at the beach. He had been her family's dentist from that time to now.

Doctor Smith pulled on a pair of gloves and began poking tools into Maxie's mouth.

"I saw Shay sitting out front behaving as always. Looked like he was engrossed in a book. He's a great little boy. I'm sure he'll become every bit the man his dad is."

Maxie pulled Doctor Smith's hands down. "Yes he is. Yes he will. He's my grandson. What else would you expect?"

"Nothing less," the doctor laughed as he held a dental instrument in each hand. "You have an uncanny way of raising wonderful, smart children, Maxie."

On the opposite side of Doctor Brown, Kerra sat on a stool next to Maxie. She smiled in pure enjoyment at the bantering between the two.

After Doctor Smith completed the procedure and Maxie stood up from the dental chair, she handed an envelope to Kerra.

"What's this?" Kerra raised her eyebrows with an inquisitive look.

Since the side of her mouth was still dead from the Novocain, Maxie held the tissue to her mouth to keep saliva from draining down her chin and spoke as clearly as she could.

"It's an invitation. If you're not busy I'll look forward to seeing you."

Kerra followed Maxie to the reception desk to make sure she was okay. Then she returned the file to Sarah to make an appointment for Maxie's next checkup. While near the waiting room she peeked around the corner to see if she could locate Maxie's grandson. Since Shay was the only child in the waiting room, she saw the blonde haired youngster that looked to be four, maybe five years old. He was dressed in surfer shorts, shirt and Crocs. He turned the pages of a book in total contentment. Kerra didn't recall ever seeing a child sit so still and content. Not even her nephews were this well behaved.

Maxie chatted with Sarah for a couple of moments and confirmed nothing had changed regarding her dental insurance. Before she left she asked Sarah to see if Kerra was available for another moment. "I'd like to introduce her to Shay," she said.

"Sure, Mrs. Brites. Be happy to."

Sarah located Kerra just outside the reception area walking toward another exam room. "If you have time, Mrs. Brites wants to see you for just another moment."

Kerra returned to the waiting room.

"Mrs. Brites? Is everything okay?" Kerra pushed a wisp of hair back behind her ear that had come loose from her hair clip.

Maxie stood with Shay next to her. "Oh, yes. Everything is fine, she said, still holding the tissue at her lip. "I wanted to introduce you to my grandson, Shay."

"Hello, Shay. I'm so happy to meet you. It's great that you came in with your grandmother to make sure she gets home okay." Kerra gave the boy a smile that caught his attention. Shay held out his hand to shake and Kerra reciprocated.

"You have pretty teeth," he said with total seriousness. Gammie told me she wanted me to meet you because I'll be coming to get my teeth checked soon. She said you might be the one to look at them."

The two released hands as Kerra continued to look down at Shay with amusement.

"She just may be correct. I would love to check your teeth and make sure they're growing well for now. But you know, you'll be losing them all at some time so your permanent teeth can grow in."

"I know! Look, I have a loose one here." Shay wiggled the tooth to the right of his front tooth back and forth.

"When this one comes out, I'm going to get some money. The tooth fairy will leave it under my pillow."

Kerra bent forward with her hands on her knees and smiled into Shay's beautiful blue eyes.

"That's what I hear," she said. "Let me know when it happens, okay?"

"I will," Shay smiled.

Maxie took Shay by the hand. "Come on Sport, we have to let Kerra get back to work." But Shay had one more question. "Miss Kerra, do you think you could come to my birthday party on Sunday at Gammie's house?"

"Uh, well I'm not sure," Kerra replied with a smile and looked toward Maxie. Maxie just lifted her shoulders and presented a sly grin.

"I'll tell you what, Shay. I'll call your gammie later for details and I will do my best to be there."

"Okay," Shay said. "If you'll do your best. Oh, and I have one more question. Are you married Miss Kerra?"

Maxie was so caught off guard with Shay's unexpected question that she spoke up immediately. "Come on Shay, we better go. We don't want Kerra to get fired because we kept her talking instead of working."

Kerra said goodbye and watched as the two disappeared from the office. She was laughing to herself about Shay's question. Why in the world would he ask such? Kerra walked from the waiting room to the break room. She reached into her pocket and pulled out the envelope that Maxie had given her. She opened it and found an invitation with directions to attend Shay's fifth birthday party at Maxie's home.

At day's end, just before Sarah locked the office door, Jason entered the building. Sarah grinned ear to ear. She and Jason had dated for a while, but what she hoped for never became a reality. Jason told her from the beginning that he wasn't looking for a serious relationship, but she believed she could change his mind.

"Hey Heartbreaker, you need to make an appointment? Don't you know how to call instead of rushing in here at the last minute?"

Jason leaned against the reception counter built higher than the long desk where Sarah sat on the opposite side. He grinned back at her. He always thought that she was very attractive with her dark blonde hair. She looked good in a swimsuit or daisy duke shorts during the times they spent boating and snorkeling together. And she turned heads when she dressed for other occasions. She even had a sense of humor that created laughter when he least expected it. But he had found a reason to break off their relationship, just like dozens of others. Dustin always told him he was nuts.

"Well, I do know I could've called, but time got away from me. I was hoping I was in time for something else."

Sarah smiled and fidgeted with the pen she held between her fingers. Maybe Jason finally realized he missed her and came to ask her out for a date. With her heart beating a little faster, she asked in anticipation: "And what would that be?"

"I'm looking for Kerra. Is she still here?"

Disappointment slid into the pit of Sarah's stomach. But she managed to keep Jason from seeing signs of it play on her face. "How do you know Kerra?" she asked, while keeping a pleasant tone.

"Met her at the pier Saturday morning while I was fishing. I wanted to invite her to a party this coming weekend."

"Actually, Kerra left a bit early today." Sarah swallowed hard and pushed her chair back from the desk. She picked up the keys that she had pulled from her purse and walked to the client side of the counter where Jason stood. Still working hard to keep her tone pleasant she said: "I need to lockup. Kerra will be here in the morning if you want to call or drop by."

Jason turned and walked to the door that Sarah held open for his exit.

"Would you do me a favor and tell her in the morning that I dropped by. And, here, give her this." It was a business card with his name and cell phone number. "Tell her to give me a call if she has time."

Sarah accepted the card from Jason. She had one just like it still in her purse. Then she couldn't hold her thoughts any longer. "You know Jason, the girl hasn't been in town too very long. You're a nice enough guy, but don't go messing with the heart and mind of a new resident who happens to be a really sweet person."

"Now Sarah, just because we didn't work out, doesn't mean I'm not supposed to keep looking."

"The thing is Jason, I don't believe you know what or who you're looking for. You can't even count the number of hearts you've left on the trail."

Sarah clutched the door knob with one hand and pointed her index finger on the other toward the parking lot. "Jason, you can go now. Office hours are over. I'll give Kerra your message."

Jason heard the sternness in Sarah's voice. "Okay, okay. I'm out of here," he said, and exited the office while Sarah controlled her emotions well enough not to slam the door.

At 6:00 p.m. Kerra walked the short distance from the cottage to the edge of the water. She carried her beach chair and a small bag with a bottle of water and a magazine. Summer tourists cleared the beaches usually between 3:30 and 4:00 p.m. to prepare themselves for the waiting lines at the most popular restaurants with views of the gulf and sunsets. With the temperature lower in the evenings and a cool breeze easing off the gulf, this was always the best time to relax and think about nothing. Kerra perched at the water's edge so she could feel the rhythm of the surf move back and forth across her feet. She created her own self styled sea sand foot massage by digging her feet into the sand and saltwater up to her ankles, then shuffled her feet slowly back and forth. Now comfortable, Kerra leaned back in the chair and closed her eyes. The sound of the surf washing gently over her feet and onto shore sometimes lulled her into a nap. And just in case that happened, she set her cell phone alarm to awaken her so she wouldn't miss the sunset. But for some reason this evening, the alarm didn't sound or Kerra slept through it. And she was dreaming that she was with Winston and their families back in Wisconsin.

They had known one another their entire lives. Winston's and Kerra's parents were all high school sweethearts who married. After Kerra and Winston were born in the same year, they grew up together. The middle of three girls, Kerra was always smart, learning words and reading quickly with the help of her older sister and mom. She never wanted help to accomplish things. Even in learning to tie her shoes. Once her big sister showed her the first time, she insisted on doing it herself until she made all the loops by herself. Her independent nature kept family and friends on their toes.

By age five Kerra informed her mom that she no longer wanted dresses or dolls. She demanded jeans and t-shirts, a cap and boots so she could help her dad with the calves at his dairy farm. The calves that she helped to name and feed were her best friends along with Winston and her twin cousins, Luke and Landon, sons of her father's sister. By age eight, Winston, Luke and Landon rode their bikes from their homes a mile away to the barn to see the calves and how they were taken care of. By age fourteen, they were all earning an allowance by helping Kerra's dad feed both the calves and milk cows, and also helped with the milking process, which were jobs that had to be accomplished in the early morning and again in the evening.

Wisconsin winters made the job difficult. Harsh cold winds pressed against the barn doors and make them next to impossible to open. Snow blew through cracks in the weathered walls and roof and created piles of snowdrifts on the barn floor and in the cow stalls. Kerra, Winston and the twins helped shovel the snow into buckets and wheelbarrows and then remove it from the barn to keep as much mud and slush down as possible.

But along with the hard work, Kerra, Winston, Luke and Landon always found ways to create fun and laughter while getting their jobs done. Inside the barn, they pitched hay into the stalls while one of them drove another around in the wheelbarrow. Or as someone scampered from a hiding place, others squeezed milk from a cow's udder in efforts to hit the moving target.

Farm life was good and fun for them. They all grew up with dreams. Her cousins became professional bull riders. Kerra went to college, and Winston continued working for Mr. Masters and dreamed of someday buying the dairy farm. But that dream had been crushed.

Suddenly Kerra bolted forward in her chair and gripped the arm rests. She tried to refocus and escape the recurring dream where she stood by Winston as he lay unconscious at the hospital two years before.

As the sun eased into the gulf, she released a heavy sigh from deep within and returned to a relaxed position in her chair. She had not noticed the tall handsome man with the paddle-board walking from the water and toward her.

"M'am, are you okay?"

Kerra, startled by the voice, sat up. "Yes, I'm fine. Thank you."

"Okay. Just checking. You seemed to be having a panic attack a few moments ago."

"Oh. No. I fell asleep and woke up startled by a crazy dream. I can't even remember it now. Funny how that happens, isn't it?"

"Yea, I know how that can be," Dustin replied in a demure manner. "I've had a few dreams like that myself."

Kerra removed her sunglasses and Dustin remembered the woman's face and the orange swimsuit. "I believe we've met before," he said.

Kerra turned her head a bit. "I believe you're right. My umbrella almost hit you in the head a couple of weeks ago."

"That's it. Any more incidents since then?"

"No. You taught me well. Thanks again."

Kerra's beach chair seat was low to the ground with the frame buried in the sand. In her attempt to stand she lost balance. Dustin grabbed her before she fell down. His attempt to keep her from falling brought her against his body. Like before, he felt a slight bolt of electricity race through his limbs, as did Kerra. For a moment they stood speechless.

Dustin made the first move and stepped backwards away from Kerra. "Sorry about that," he said. "Glad you're okay."

"Thanks," Kerra replied as she composed herself.

"You take care."

"Sure thing."

Kerra turned to pull her chair from its sink hole at the water's edge as Dustin walked to the water hose on the boardwalk. After rinsing the salt and sand from his paddle-board, he let the cold water wash over his head and down his body. He didn't want to feel the sensation that the woman by the water had caused when her body accidentally fell against his. He didn't want to think about the possibility that there was someone he could be attracted to. He already had enough emotions to keep under control for good job performance and being a dad. Carrying the scars of battlefields wasn't just about him. The scars extended to everyone he loved, just like his grandpa Claude and dad had told him. A number of his battle buddies were already divorced and struggling to cope in the aftermath of everything they had survived in the war zones. There was no greater truth than the fact that war veterans leave one battlefield just to return home to a different kind. Wives, fiancés, and girlfriends had let go of good men that had been emotionally and physically broken due to circumstances out of their control. It wasn't always the woman's fault. He knew those that had tried to keep their families together, but the drinking and Post Traumatic

Stress issues of their war torn husbands had become more than they and their children could take. And of course, there were those that didn't want to try. Young women who barely knew, yet married, young military men before they deployed, were not mature or capable enough to handle a returning wounded warrior. Especially those with missing limbs or severe body burns from incidents by improvised explosive devices or rocket propelled grenades. Dustin often thought of his buddy that had spent months at Walter Reed Hospital located in Washington D.C. before it became known as Walter Reed National Military Medical Center moved to Bethesda, Maryland. His friend was a double amputee with a young wife and baby.

Unfortunately the young wife had looked at him and said, "You expect me to live with this?" Then she left the room. The wife filed divorce papers and signed full custody of the baby to the soldier. His mother quit her job to take care of her son and grandson. Dustin called and checked on his friend every few weeks. He was doing well with his son at the center of his life. And a new relationship was forming with a friend from high school that visited him on a regular basis.

But Dustin wasn't ready to believe he could add another person to his own life, although he knew success stories existed. He didn't want to gamble on his ability to be the man that a girlfriend would expect, or to handle the emotional stress that could be caused if he did fall in love, but the other party didn't feel the same, or they couldn't handle his mood swings. He now chose to play life safe because he was far too familiar with stressors and triggers from personal experience and observations that lead to depression and negative reactions even towards family members on unexpected bad days.

In the light of a full moon and lights from the boardwalk, Kerra strolled back toward the cottage. She was surprised that she couldn't shake the feeling from the touch of the tall handsome man that she had now seen twice. He sounded mild and truly concerned about her being okay. Again, she had thanked him, but never introduced herself or asked his name.

"Well," she thought to herself, "If he's a local, I'll probably see him again."

When Kerra arrived at her front door, Kitten, the designated name, was waiting. The yet to be identified male or female cat had become more trusting. After Kerra opened the door, for the first time, Kitten scampered inside with her.

"Well, well," Kerra mused, "are you finally going to be my friend?"

"Meow," Kitty responded as though answering yes to Kerra's question.

After providing water and food for Kitten, Kerra put the fur ball inside the bathroom. She grabbed her purse and drove to Wal-Mart to purchase a flea collar, flea powder, kitty litter, a box and a carrier to easily transport Kitten to the veterinarian as soon as she obtained an appointment. Even for a Monday night, summer tourist traffic eased along bumper to bumper. Young people in cars, trucks, and rental scooters yelled joyous commotions and honked horns at one another. People of all ages walked along each side of Front Beach Road carrying six-packs, twelve-packs, and grocery bags from small stores close to their condominiums and hotels. Kerra finally made it to the street where she turned into Walmart's parking lot. After locating a parking place beneath a light 'out in the back forty', a term she'd learned from her dad about parking a great distance from an entry point, her phone chirped with a text message. Kerra touched the screen and read her mom's note. "Just letting you know I'm thinking about you. Also, have you found a doctor yet?" Kerra typed a return message: "Love you, too. Give dad a hug for me. No doctor yet. Will talk later. At store."

"Mom, Mom, Mom," Kerra whispered to herself. "Please stop worrying."

Kerra held her head up, smiled and made eye contact with everyone in her path as she walked briskly from her car to the doors of Walmart. She had always heard that making eye contact was the best way to deter anyone that might be stalking women in parking lots. It was a sign of strength and intimidating for someone on the prowl. Kerra accepted the push cart from the smiling greeter inside the entrance and set out seeking the pet department. On the way she slowed down when she saw the children's toy department.

"Hmmmm," she said quietly. "Guess I should meander through these aisles for a few minutes and find a birthday gift for Shay." But she had no idea what to purchase. She didn't even know the boy or what his interests were. Kerra could only assume that Maxie had invited her to Shay's birthday party to be nice and help her to feel more at home in the community and help her gain friends and acquaintances. Kerra pulled her cell phone from the small purse that hung across her shoulder and pressed the phone number for her older sister. Her boys were five and eight. After a couple of rings, Lori answered the phone: "Hey Sis, what's up? Mom says you're lovin' your new residence and job."

"Yea, I'm pretty happy. I'm hoping all of you will visit sometime in the future."

Kerra shifted herself and the push cart from the middle of the aisle to the side to allow space for another shopper.

"We want to," Lori said. "It's a matter of time and money. You know how it goes. By the way, have you found a doctor yet?"

Kerra sighed and turned to fidget with the small super hero figurines sitting on the shelf in front of her. "Not yet. I'm researching doctors here. I want to be sure I find the best one."

"Please don't wait too long," Lori pleaded. "We all need you. You had a pretty bad concussion in that car accident. You need to keep those headaches under control."

"I know, I know," Kerra said. "I love you, too."

There was a quick pause before Kerra spoke again to her sister. "Lori, have you heard anything lately about Winston? Mom told me that he was back in the hospital. Then I had a dream that I was back sitting with him while he was unconscious."

"As far as I know, his family is taking care of him as best they can. It hasn't been easy on them. His folks talk to our folks now and then. You know how close they've always been."

"I know," Kerra responded. "Mom told me that Winston had been asking for me. That he wanted to know where I was. I asked her if I had done enough to help, or had I been a coward to leave to try and start up my life again."

"Hey, Sis, take the load off," Lori said softly. "You've done nothing wrong. You have the right to try to find your own way through the cow patties of life."

Kerra couldn't help but laugh. "Cow patties of life," she repeated to Lori. "Haven't heard that one in a while. So, let's get off the cow patties and I'll ask a question I really need help with. What kind of birthday present do I give a five year old boy that I don't know?"

"Why would you be buying for a child you don't know?"

"He's the grandson of one of my clients at work. She invited me to his birthday party on Sunday."

"Well, that's strange. Why would she do that?"

"I'm guessing because she knows I'm new to the area. She's a sweetheart and wants to be a friend."

"Oh, okay," Lori responded. "Mmmm, just get a gift card or give some cash in a birthday card. Kids love money and shopping. Can't go wrong with cash or gift cards."

"Sounds like the best idea." Kerra's tone changed from near melancholy to jovial. "Thanks Sis, I love you. Give the kids a hug for me."

"Love you and will do. They miss you."

"Miss them, too. Tell them I'll skype with them soon."

Kerra pressed the End Call button and made her way to the pet department and found the items she needed for Kitten. She located a birthday card to put cash for Shay and then made her way to the checkout where she picked up the most recent copy of *Woman's World*.

CHAPTER SEVEN

On Tuesday morning, Kerra completed her routine stretching and yoga, then took a cup of green tea and yogurt to the table. Kitten, who had received an unwanted bath the night before, flea powder, and a collar wrapped his or her self around Kerra's ankles. It was good to have company in the cottage.

After arriving at work the first person Kerra saw was Sarah. She was already busy working with files and the computer. But she didn't look up with her usual bubbly greeting. She appeared in the depths of total concentration with no trace of a smile.

"Hi Sarah. Are you okay this morning?" Kerra asked with concern.

Sarah's head pounded as she continued typing. "I have a headache from drinking a little too much wine last night."

"Ooooh, I know how that can feel! Can I get you a glass of water or orange juice? Rehydrating can help relieve the headache a little."

Sarah stopped typing and held up a large bottle of spring water. "Thanks, but I brought some with me. I've just got to get through this day. By the way, someone left a personal message for you yesterday after you left the office."

Kerra couldn't imagine who would be leaving messages. "Really? I don't know anyone that should be leaving me any personal messages? That's weird."

Sarah handed Kerra the business card from Jason. "He wants to know if you'll give him a call."

"Do you happen to know Jason?"

"Oh yes. Pretty well. Most of the hometown girls do. And some who have visited our beach city and returned to their own home towns. He's a nice, good looking guy. But beware! He likes to leave a path of broken hearts. Can't seem to make up his mind what color hair, body style, or IQ he prefers in a woman."

"Well, Sarah, I appreciate your sharing that with me. We met while he was fishing at the city pier last Saturday and I was taking a walk. We had a conversation. He showed me how to cast, and later that evening I drove my own car to meet him at Harpoon Harry's for dinner. But he's really not my type. Although you're right, he's nice and good looking."

Kerra cocked her head and looked at Sarah who was almost drowning herself with water.

"Is that why you drank too much wine last night? Because you have a thing for Jason and he stopped here looking for me?"

Sarah almost choked. "Uhhh, well, I guess. Dumb, huh?"

"Honey, if he doesn't have sense enough to know what a catch you are then he doesn't deserve you. Hang in there. Don't let him get the best of you."

"You're right. I can't believe I allowed him to press my buttons enough to do something so stupid to myself. Lesson learned."

Sarah held her head between her hands as both women laughed and agreed to find a way to pull something on Jason.

"Oh, before you unlock the doors, I need to ask one more question. Can you recommend a veterinarian that's close by? The kitten has decided it likes me. I need to take it for an examination and shots."

Sarah told Kerra about Dr. Lafountain located a half mile from their office.

"Thanks. I'll call and make an appointment during lunch time."

Kerra also planned on calling Jason.

The office closed from twelve to one for lunch. Kerra called Dr. Lafountain and arranged for a Saturday morning appointment for Kitten. Then she dialed Jason's number.

"This is Jason. Leave a message and number. I'll hit you back as soon as possible."

"Hi Jason, this is Kerra. Sarah told me you stopped by yesterday. Sorry I was already gone for the day. I'm on lunch break here at the office until one o'clock. Otherwise you can call my cell number after office hours. You'll see the number on your caller ID."

Kerra dropped her phone inside her uniform pocket and joined the rest of the staff in the break room. A plethora of food was pulled from lunch bags. She pulled her own organic green salad garnished with salmon from the refrigerator, then placed a cup of water with a green tea bag in the microwave.

"Girl, you eat too healthy. You make the rest of us look bad," Vicki said jokingly. "It looks good, but I guess throwing an unhealthy lunch together is quicker than a healthy one."

Kerra took no offense and smiled. "It's just a matter of getting into a routine," she said. Just as she sat down at the table to eat, her cell phone vibrated inside her pocket. It was Jason.

"Hi, what's up?" she said without calling his name aloud. There was no reason for everyone knowing her business for rumors to build on.

"Sorry I missed your call earlier. We were finishing up maintenance on some equipment. How are things with you today?"

"Well, thank you. Trying to finish lunch before I return to teeth cleaning."

"I won't hold you then. I just wondered if you had plans for the weekend."

"Let me call you back on that. Can I call you after I leave work?"

"Sure. I'll look forward to it."

"Okay. Bye, bye."

Kerra dropped the phone back inside her pocket, and then poked her fork around in her greens and salmon. She noticed the women at the table grinning at one another like Cheshire cats.

"*What?*" she asked sharply while trying to hold back a laugh. She wanted them all to believe she had been on a serious business call.

"We are nosy women, you know," said Lois. We can tell one kind of phone call from another. Had to be somebody from around here already hitting on you.

Kerra and Sarah grinned and lifted their eyebrows at one another.

"Well one of your community's most eligible and desirable bachelors seems interested in me." Kerra said with a sly grin and taunting voice.

"Who, who!" The three women sitting with Kerra and Sarah sounded like a bunch of owls.

"It must be Dustin!" Vicki popped up. "Oh girl, how lucky you are!"

"Nope. Haven't met a Dustin. What makes him so special?" Kerra took another bite of greens and salmon.

"He's just the hunkiest hunk and war hero in Bay County. Works at Fire & Beach Rescue," said Lois.

"No, it's not a Dustin. It's a Jason from Fire & Beach Rescue."

The women turned silent with wide eyes toward Sarah and suddenly found their beverages to swallow or food to chew.

Sarah laughed and slapped her hands on the table. "Hey girls! I already knew. Kerra and I have talked. I've given her the scoop on Mr. Heartbreaker and I'm pretty sure Kerra will hold her own with him.

"Ooooo, this should be interesting," Vicki said, as she moved toward the sink to clean her dishes.

"I'm sure Jason has a good heart," Kerra said with sincerity as she closed the top on her food container. "He's just so used to girls being taken by his charm and good looks that he's looking for a challenge. The thing is, as I told Sarah, he is cute and sweet, but not my type. And I want to let him down easy."

"You'll be the first," Lois said. "He's usually the one that's giving the easy let down. He'll sure be surprised."

"Well sometimes it takes something unexpected to keep a person from taking things for granted about themselves or others," Kerra replied.

The others agreed. After everyone walked in different directions from the break room Kerra's own comment took her back to Wisconsin where she learned from personal experience never to take anything for granted. Only her understanding didn't come from some silly boy, girl challenges. Her understanding came from an unexpected event that occurred in an instant. An event that was never supposed to happen to her or someone she dearly loved.

It was two years ago, 2009. She and Winston were driving to a concert in Eau Claire, Wisconsin. Winston still worked for her dad at the dairy farm. He was no longer the scrawny boy she once fished and climbed trees with or chased around the barn with a pail of water to throw at him before he splashed her. He was all muscle from working for her dad in the hayfield, moving hay bales that fed the cows, and working with hammers and other tools that kept fences and the barn mended. He also helped directly with the cows and milking process, made silage from hay, and tended the cornfield and soy beans.

There was a time they believed they would marry and carry on the farm, but their first attempted grown-up kiss deterred that belief.

"Uh, did that feel right to you?" Winston had asked Kerra.

"I can't say I'm feeling comfortable or with a burst of fireworks going off in my brain," she told him.

They both laughed and settled on the fact that they were more brother and sister than a pair meant for the intimacy of marriage. And inside her heart, Kerra had already realized that she didn't want to be glued to farm life. With her parents' blessings, she entered the dental care program at Chippewa Valley Technical College in Eau Claire, Wisconsin, twenty-three miles from her Augusta home. Two years later she graduated with her degree and obtained a job with a dental office in Eau Claire.

When Kerra and Winston found themselves without dates for special occasions, or they just wanted to hang out and catch up, they called one another. Their young lives couldn't have been more fulfilling. They dreamed and talked about all that was ahead in their futures. Winston believed that someday he would buy the milk dairy from Kerra's dad. Kerra focused on saving money so she and her mom could go together on a Mediterranean cruise.

Kerra still lived at her parents' home where she paid rent, because she insisted. Winston bought an older model mobile home and placed it on a piece of ground his folks deeded to him as a high school graduation gift. He would build a house there someday. His old pickup truck came from money he had saved from earnings at the dairy from age fourteen to seventeen. Kerra had saved enough money by the time she went to college that she bought a 1995 Camry. Having learned about keeping up farm vehicles and equipment, she knew how to keep her own car running well. She understood the importance of frequent oil and filter changes, checking transmission and brake fluids, air in the tires, and most important how to change a tire. She learned this on her own at age fifteen after going to the hayfield to find her dad.

She had driven his pickup truck without realizing that the left front tire had a slow leak from a nail puncture. After taking a lunch bag to her dad, she returned to the truck to see the tire flat against the dirt. Always accepting a challenge, she found a jack and spare in the truck bed. Forty minutes later she was back at the house with a big grin on her face.

Kerra drove her Camry the night she and Winston went to Eau Claire for the concert. A Toby Keith CD played in the new stereo she had had installed a few weeks before. They were chatting and laughing at each other's comical experiences from the prior work week.

"So is that stubborn old milk cow, Big Red, still up to her usual antics?" Kerra asked.

"Nothing's changed since you chose to help people keep their teeth in good order instead of keeping with the good life of dairy farming," Winston replied with a chuckle. "She's still keeping me on my toes and causing traffic jams."

Kerra laughed. She never forgot being taught at six years old that every milk cow was trained from a calf to learn which stall to enter for feeding and milking. When they were brought from pasture every evening the cows automatically strolled to their stall like school children to specific desks. Then along came Red who sometimes showed her independence much like Kerra. On occasion she wanted to change up the boring daily routine and choose another stall. Inside the barn Red created a traffic jam when she stopped and refused to move while deciding which stall she wanted to enter. During her selection process she had to be coerced and prodded until she reluctantly entered her own stall. Red had another antic during the morning and evening milking process. After milking lines were attached to her udders, she watched from the corner of her eye until Winston walked away and then she would pick up her rear leg and kick until she disconnected the milking unit. When she pulled the shenanigan, Winston rushed back to pick up the line and reconnect it to Red before it sucked hay from the floor and into the milking system and caused a clog.

"Red may be stubborn, but she's still my favorite," Kerra said with a laugh. "She makes for fun conversation and the best thing she's done is produce her sweet calf Rosie."

After Kerra halted the car at a red traffic light, she began telling Winston about the elderly farmer that came to the dental office for a tooth extraction. He wore overalls scattered with holes and a shirt that was also aged. When the man sat down and Kerra leaned the dental chair back, one of the holes appeared in a place below his pants zipper. Unfortunately for Kerra, the man wore no underwear and she received a view of the family jewels. She immediately placed several dental napkins across his lap before she placed one around his neck. As Kerra completed the story Winston laughed so hard that tears flushed his eyes.

Then it happened. As Kerra moved slowly forward with a green traffic light, the car to the right drove through a red light and plowed into the passenger side of the Camry and sent it spinning.

Kerra woke up in a hospital bed with her family standing around her. The first face she focused on was her dad who stood at the foot of the bed. Her mom was to her left and both sisters to her right.

"What's going on, Dad?" she asked in a raspy, breaking voice.

"Hey, Honey, you're okay. There was a car accident. Do you remember?"

Kerra closed her eyes and lay quiet and still.

"Winston and I," she paused. "We were headed to the concert in Eau Claire. We were laughing." Tears flowed down Kerra's face. "What did I do? What did I do?"

"Honey, you didn't do anything wrong. Another driver's brakes gave way and they couldn't stop at the red light on their side. They crashed into the passenger side of your car."

"Winston, how's Winston?" Kerra's face became drawn with panic.

The family members all looked at one another seeking who would speak first. Kerra turned her face toward her mom. "Tell me, Mom, now! How is Winston?"

Sylvia smiled weakly and patted her daughter's shaking hand.

"Winston is in intensive care. He's still unconscious and has some broken bones. He has some bleeding on his brain and emergency surgery was required. But the doctors believe he'll pull through."

"He will be fine. I know he will. Winston is strong and strong-willed. When can I see him?"

"Only his family can visit ICU. But we will ask if you can go in. Although it may not be good for you right now. Just try and be patient. Let's see how the next few days go." Sylvia gently brushed Kerra's hair back from her forehead and the bandage that covered a cut above her left eye.

With medical monitors attached to her, Kerra had slept for the past seven hours. She was not yet realizing the bruising to her own body, the displaced shoulder or the concussion she had experienced.

While Kerra was deep in thought about the accident, Sarah entered the breakroom.

"Hey girl. You okay? You look like you're in a daze. What's up?"

"Oh, sorry. I'm fine. Just thinking about family and friends back in Wisconsin. I'll be right there."

"Okay, you tell me if I can do anything," Sarah said.

"I promise I will. Okay back to work. People are waiting." Kerra rubbed her fingers across her forehead. She hadn't experienced a bad headache in a while. But since the concussion they sometimes came on without warning accompanied by some dizziness. She couldn't pretend any longer that the problem didn't exist. Just because she left one place where it all began didn't mean the problem would stay behind. It was time to find a doctor.

CHAPTER EIGHT

On Saturday morning, Dustin was at work at the station while Hugh and Shay went to Lake Powell to fish and Maxie wandered the aisles of Party Shop to select items for birthday bags. Ten children were attending Shays birthday party at 1:00 p.m. on Sunday, along with their parents. Most of them were children of crew members from Beach Rescue. Others were neighborhood children.

Because Shay, just like his dad, loved the water and sea life, Maxie had already arranged for Smiley the dolphin mascot to drop by from Gulf World. Shay began learning about the gulf and sea life after Dustin returned home from the Army. He, Maxie and Hugh took beach walks with Shay, collected sea shells together and often visited St Andrews State Park to search for star fish and sand dollars that had washed onto shore. Along the bay edges, especially in sea weed, they discovered small shrimp, oysters, and small crabs carrying their shell homes on their backs.

Once after a day's excursion Dustin brought home a crab the size of a quarter and while Shay watched in amazement, Dustin painted its shell green and put his and Shay's initials on it. Speedy lived in Shay's room in a square plastic container with a vented lid with a friend that was brought home and painted soon after Speedy.

Shay was three when his dad and granddad put a life jacket on him for a trip in Hugh's boat to the bay. For the first time Shay saw dolphins jumping and playing in the wild. After that, he wanted everything dolphin. He wasn't old enough yet to swim with the dolphins at Gulf World. But it wouldn't be long.

Maxie already had Mylar balloon shaped dolphins, sea turtles, and starfish to hang from the ceiling in the new sun room across the rear of the house. Outside the new sunroom was a new swimming pool and hot tub. Shay was told that the pool was his fifth birthday present so that friends and he could enjoy really fun birthday parties for a long time to come.

The hot tub was more for Dustin to relax with the heat and jets to help soothe the aches and pains of a body battered more than he would ever let on to anyone except the VA doctors for the purpose of his disability ratings.

At Party Shop, Maxie finished the selections for Shay's party and pushed the buggy to the cashier.

"I think I have everything I need," she told the associate. "Eleven of everything. Please help me make sure."

The associate counted each of the items: goody bags, yo-yos, whistles, floating rubber ducks, silly putty, and water pistols.

"My grandson will be five tomorrow," Maxie announced. "Have to make sure the children attending have something fun to take home."

Maxie paid for the items that included a happy birthday table cloth, napkins, plates, and plastic forks and spoons. She had already purchased dolphin, sea turtle, and whale floats for the kids to use in the new swimming pool. Her last stop was at her favorite grocery store.

She purchased hamburgers and hotdogs for grilling on Sunday along with condiments and chips, then pushed the grocery cart from the store and placed everything in her car trunk. Maxie returned to the store's bakery for the sheet cake she had ordered more than a week before. The smell of baking breads, cookies, and cakes drifted from the bakery and through the store. Joann, the bakery manager who had known Maxie for twenty-five years, met Maxie at the counter with the cake.

"Well, what do you think?"

Joann smiled proudly as she held the cake so Maxie could see the white frosting trimmed with blue sea frosting, candy palm trees, boats, dolphins and starfish.

"It's perfect Joann. You've always provided exactly what I ordered all the way back to Dustin. Thank you so much."

"And how is Dustin?" Joann asked. She had known him since he was just a boy.

"He's come a long way. He's adjusted well, loves his job and being a dad. All he needs now is a good woman. Although he doesn't believe he has the ability to give any more love, and worse than that, believes he doesn't deserve love after being in combat."

"Oh Maxie, you gotta let things like that go. If it's meant to be, it'll be."

"Yeah, you're right, Joann. Thanks for the reminder and thanks for asking about Dustin. I'll see you later."

Maxie paid for the cake and returned to the car. She secured it safely for the quick drive home. Just as she settled behind the steering wheel with her seatbelt secured, her cell phone rang. The number with no name attached looked unfamiliar with an out-of-state area code. She could only think of one possibility.

"Hello. This is Maxie Brites," she answered.

"Hi, Mrs. Brites, this is Kerra Masters from the dental office. I just wanted to let you know that I'll be seeing you and Shay tomorrow for his birthday. I want to thank you for including me. I really appreciate your thoughtfulness."

As Kerra spoke, Maxie silently said, "yes, yes, yes," and smiled with thorough happiness from ear to ear. After Kerra finished her sentences, Maxie immediately responded.

"Kerra, I'm so happy you're coming. And I know Shay will be glad to see you. We just want you to know you have friends and extended family here in Panama City Beach since you're so far away from your own family."

"That is just so sweet of you. Again, I really appreciate your thoughtfulness. I'll see you tomorrow."

Maxie sang her favorite old country tune all the way home, "I'm The Happiest Girl in the Whole USA..."

On Sunday morning Kitten, now determined to be a girl and with a clean bill of health from Dr. Lafountain, lay curled on the pillow next to Kerra. The morning sun cast light through the slits of the blinds in the bedroom. "No sense in wasting daylight," Kerra said as she stroked Kitten across the top of the head. "You keep relaxing. I'm going for a walk."

By 7:00 a.m. Kerra was strolling along the beach at the edge of its gentle swaying surf. Its rhythmic washing back and forth against the shore was hypnotic. This morning the water met at a line connecting emerald green and deep blue. Where the two colors joined depended on how close sand bars were to the top of the water for the reflection of the sun. Seaweed had washed onto shore during the night and lay in batches that looked like long brown beards or long hair in great need of a de-frizzing conditioner. Seagulls called out their greetings and dove for small fish swimming in schools in shallow water.

Kerra examined sea shells, picking up one here and there as she strolled slowly in bare feet and wearing a pair of athletic shorts with a swimsuit top. She carried a plastic bag for disposing of trash that she came across floating in the water or laying on the sand. The white sand still had tracks from the city vehicles that drove through in the evenings just before sunset to pick up trash from receptacles and any beach chairs, umbrellas or canopy tents that people had a tendency to leave where they had placed them. The "Let's Keep Our Beaches Clean" ordinance stated that no matter what a person left on the beach in the evenings, it would not be there the next morning. A new day opened with the offering of the best from the most beautiful beaches in the world.

At the half-mile point, Kerra turned to stroll back to the cottage. Others were now finding their way to the beach to exercise, relax with books, and play throughout the day. Others placed kayaks in the water. There were couples with the double seats and there were the single ones, both men and women. Paddle boarders on their knees and also standing maneuvered in the water with their oars. Kerra had been thinking about finding a place to take lessons to learn both sports. She was learning about all the endless opportunities that were available for a wonderful life, but then she always returned to her guilt about Winston. If he couldn't enjoy the life he always wanted, why should she be deserving of moving forward with learning new things and having fun?

Kerra returned to the cottage trying to force the doors to close on any negative thoughts. "This is going to be a good day," she said to herself. "And it's time for breakfast." Within minutes, a glass of fresh squeezed orange juice, a soft boiled egg and a piece of wheat toast were on the table of the screened patio with the most recent copy of *Woman's World*. As Kerra nibbled at the food, she perused through the magazine and came to a page with a piece called: "A Moment for You." It read: *'You've come so far! You've made progress you haven't acknowledged, developed talents you haven't tallied, come up with solutions you've shrugged off the credit for, made dreams come true—and set more in motion. Count your accomplishments. It's time to be proud of who you are!'* The words seemed a message from the universe giving her permission to be happy with herself.

Before Kerra pressed the phone number for her mom, a call was already coming in from Wisconsin. "Good morning, Mom!"

"Good morning! How are you this morning?"

"I'm wonderful. Already had my walk and breakfast. I was about to call you when the phone rang."

Kerra told her mom about Kitten and the clean bill of health and her plans to check into kayak and paddle boarding lessons.

"I'm going to a birthday party for a five year old today," she said. "I'm looking forward to it since I'm away from the kids there at home."

Kerra told her mom about the straight forward amusing Maxie and the invitation.

"Maybe she has a handsome son she's secretly planning to introduce you to," Sylvia said.

"I don't think so Mom. She's just a really nice lady who wants to make me feel at home in the community." Kitten strolled onto the patio. The cat meowed a few times and jumped onto Kerra's lap.

"Here, say hello to Sylvia." Kerra placed the phone to Kitten's mouth just as another meow escaped. "Good girl," she said and laughed.

Kerra put the phone back to her ear. "So what do you think about my cat that speaks on command?"

"Very smart, it seems," Sylvia said.

"So Mom, any update on Winston?"

"Actually his mom called and told me he received the post card you sent him from the beach. She said he grinned ear to ear. He had her pin the card to the wall in his room. He wants to know why you haven't called since you went to Florida. Is there anything I can tell him for you?"

Kerra thought for a moment. "No. Just tell him I think of him every day and I love him." Kerra kept her voice in an upbeat tone. "And I'll call him soon."

"Okay, Honey. I'll visit with him today and let him know."

"Thanks mom. Give him and his folks a hug for me." Kerra gently stroked Kitten from the top of her head to the end of her tail.

"I need to ask one more thing," said Sylvia. "Are you having any headaches?"

"No. Not a one," Kerra said. She didn't want to worry her mom. "I'm actually going to talk to Mrs. Brites today at the party to see if she can recommend good doctors in the area. They have lived here all their lives so I'm sure she can provide good info."

Kerra knew she wasn't going to ask Mrs. Brites about doctors, but she knew that saying so would get her off the hook with her mom.

"Sounds good. Let me know, okay?" Sylvia said.

"I will Mom. No worries. Tell everyone hello and I send my love."

After completing the call, Kerra cleaned her breakfast dishes, refreshed Kitten's food, and entered the shower. Sara Evan's song, "Born to Fly," played through the cottage stereo speakers while Kerra washed her hair and sang along.

Maxie's house was located only minutes from the cottage. It was an older home on a slight hill with a vague view of the gulf. Kerra parked next to the curb near the address at five minutes to one. Other cars filled the double driveway. A wide walkway with manicured grass on each side led to the small porch with an overhang of the square built house with large windows on each side and a second story. Flowering Pink Crepe Myrtle trees grew in the middle of each side of the yard, and Knockout roses bloomed beneath the windows. Outdoor stairs led to a screened balcony that extended from the side of the house at the upper level. An American flag flew from a pole attached to one of the columns that held up the roof over the small porch.

Sounds of children escaped from the back yard to the front as Kerra knocked on the door. She was not surprised when Sarah greeted her. Maxie had provided an invitation to her the same day as she did Kerra, along with Lois and Vicki for their children.

"Hey girlfriend, come on in," Sarah said with her natural glowing smile. "Good to see you made it. You'll have fun. Maxie is the hostess with the mostess. Lois and Vicki arrived with their kids just before you. They're in the backyard. The kids couldn't wait to get in the new pool."

"This is beautiful!" Kerra commented, while looking around the space that created a large open family, dining and kitchen area.

"I owe it all to my son and husband," Maxie said as she strolled in from the sun room located outside the kitchen. Kerra was admiring the new cream and brown granite counter tops.

"Hey Mrs. Brites. What a lucky lady you are. And you must have some wonderful large family meals here with this beautiful table and chairs."

"Well, first off, drop the Mrs. Brites," said Maxie, as she reached her arms toward Kerra to give her a hug. "I'm now your friend not just a dental client. And second, that table and ten chairs belonged to my mother. I refinished it not long ago. I hope to someday fill all those chairs up on holidays and other special times. But right now I'm lacking a daughter-in-law, a son-in-law and a few more grandchildren."

"Hey ladies, are you going to join the party?"

"We're on our way," Maxie replied. "Kerra, this is my husband, Hugh."

"Hello, Kerra. You must be the new girl at the dentist office that I've been hearing so much about. Glad you could join us today."

Hugh Brites and Kerra exchanged smiles and handshakes as Kerra expressed her appreciation.

"And I'm not Mr. Brites, he told her. That was my father. You can call me Hugh."

"Okay, Hugh," she said, "done deal."

Before the small group completed the walk through the kitchen to enter the sunroom, Kerra spied an interesting looking framed flag on the wall. It had a red border with a white insert and a blue star in the center of the white. She hesitated a moment. "What's this flag? It's different from anything I've seen before."

"Oh," said Maxie. "That's called a blue star service flag. It was created during World War I by a dad that had two sons serving in combat. People took up the symbol to hang in their windows. The number of blue stars on the white represented the number of loved ones serving on the front lines. It's a piece of history mostly lost until the Afghanistan Iraq wars started."

"What an interesting piece of history," Kerra said. "Do you have someone in your family serving now?" she asked.

"We did have," Maxie replied with a smile. "You ready to go outside and meet some others?"

"Absolutely!" Kerra followed Maxie.

Inside the 12 x 20 screened sun room, ceiling fans with tropical blades spun round and round. The dolphin, starfish and other sea life Mylar balloons hung from the ceiling. Two picnic tables were decorated with bright colored table cloths with HAPPY BIRTHDAY around the edges. One table for the children had goodie bags at each place setting, and the other was for the adults. Kerra continued to follow Maxie to the backyard where children laughed and splashed in the swimming pool. Parents, including Vicki and Lois, sat on the pool's edge to keep a sharp eye on the children. Maxie introduced Kerra to a couple of moms of children from the neighborhood. She also introduced her to a couple of wives of crew members that worked with Dustin at beach rescue.

Shay was about to jump off the diving board when he spotted Kerra standing with Maxie. He yelled and waved. "Watch me Miss Kerra. Watch me!"

Kerra watched as the five year old took on the water like a fish. After his cannon ball into the pool, he swam to the step ladder at the side of the pool and pulled himself up. "Did you bring your swimsuit, Miss Kerra?"

"No, Shay, I'm afraid I didn't. But I sure enjoyed watching your cannon ball off the board. You seem to be quite an expert already."

"Oh, no, not really. But I will be when I get older. My dad is teaching me. Gammie says I have talent like my dad."

"Well that sounds exciting, Shay. Maybe you'll grow up to be a part of the Olympics."

"I know!" Shay replied bright eyed. My dad almost went to the Olympics one time."

Out of the pool, Shay took hold of Kerra's hand. "Come with me. I want you to meet my dad. He's cooking hamburgers and hotdogs for everybody over at the grill."

Shay led Kerra to another part of the back yard where a large gas grill was part of a semi complete outdoor kitchen. Palm trees in a group of three and some elephant ears gave the area a tropical look. A wooden swing hanging from a frame and several chairs were placed together beneath a canopy tent. As Shay and Kerra walked closer to the grill where smoke wafted through the air, she saw the backs of two men. The one cooking was about six foot two and lean. The other one appeared around five-ten.

"Hey, Dad, I want you to meet someone."

Both men turned and Kerra stopped in her tracks.

Jason faced her. She had called him back on Friday evening and turned down his invitation to a weekend party. She had not asked him anything about the party he had invited her to because she already knew she had plans for Shay's. But this must have been the party he was talking about. And next to Jason stood the tall handsome man she'd met twice at the beach without ever learning his name.

"Well, Shay!" Jason said, "Is this your new girl friend?"

"Nooo, Jason, she's not my girlfriend. She's Gammie's new friend from the dentist office. I wanted to introduce her to dad."

Kerra shifted her eyes from Jason to Dustin. They stared at one another unable to move. Dustin finally spoke the first words following Shay's.

"Hi, I'm Dustin Brites. Shay's dad. Nice to meet you."

"I'm Kerra Masters," nice to meet you, too.

Dustin extended his hand to Kerra. She slowly reciprocated. As their hands locked for a courteous shake, they felt a physical sensation that both wanted to deny, and quickly released the grip.

Kerra shifted her eyes back to Jason. "Hi Jason, good to see you again."

"Same here," Jason said, as he lifted the beer that he held in his hand.

Shay still held to Kerra's hand. She was fine with that. Dustin looked at Jason then back at Kerra. You two know each other?

"You could say that," Jason said. "We met briefly on the fishing pier a couple of weeks ago."

Suddenly Kerra felt uncomfortable and embarrassed. Here was the tall, handsome bronze stranger in front of her that her beach umbrella had almost smacked. She had felt somewhat of an electric current when her body touched his that day on the beach when she fell against him. Their handshake sent another current through her. And Shay was his son. Where was Shay's mother? And here was Jason that she had met for dinner. This was more than uncomfortable. Feeling overwhelmed and confused, Kerra smiled and looked down at Shay as she struggled to keep herself calm.

"Well, Shay, I appreciate your bringing me out here to see your beautiful backyard and to meet your dad. What do you say about going back to the pool? I don't believe I've met your mom yet?"

The two men were still looking toward Shay and Kerra. Dustin was about to speak when Shay responded. "Oh, I don't have a mom. She died when I was just a baby."

Kerra didn't know what to say. All she wanted to do was run. How could she have ended up in such an awkward situation? She finally knelt down to Shay's level.

"Oh, Shay, sweetie, I am so sorry. I didn't know."

"It's okay," Dustin said as he walked closer. "It's a long story. Here, let me help you up."

Kerra accepted Dustin's extended hand and let him pull her from kneeling in front of Shay. The touch between the two created the same current.

Kerra looked up into Dustin's eyes. "I'm so embarrassed," she said quietly. "I think I should go now."

Then she looked down at Shay and squeezed his hand gently.

"Come on Shay, I'll walk you back to the swimming pool to play with your friends. You don't want to miss your own birthday party."

Shay held to Kerra's hand as they strolled back to the pool where the others were still playing and laughing. When they were next to the pool, Shay said, "Watch Miss Kerra." And he dove into the deep end of the water.

Kerra, still a bit dumb founded, located Maxie in the kitchen. She was arranging condiments on trays.

"Hi, Kerra. I hope you're enjoying yourself."

"Hi Maxie. Shay took me to meet his dad. I was a bit shocked. I'm so sorry about the loss of his wife. It must be difficult on him and Shay." Kerra leaned against the counter next to where Maxie was slicing tomatoes for the burgers.

"Oh Honey." Maxie laid down the knife, then washed and dried her hands. "There's a long story behind this. Dustin and Shay's mom were not married, they…"

Before Maxie finished the sentence, Dustin walked in holding an aluminum pan full of grilled hotdogs and hamburgers. "Mom, where would you like these?"

Kerra moved from where she leaned against the kitchen counter and walked toward the living room.

"Here, just sit them here on top of the stove. I'll cover them in aluminum foil."

Kerra watched as mother and son maneuvered around the stove.

"I apologize," she said. "But I can't stay." Kerra pulled the envelope from her purse with the card and money for Shay. "Please give this to Shay for me."

Maxie and Dustin both looked at her. "Are you okay, honey?" Maxie asked.

"I have a slight headache. Sometimes they turn into migraines. I don't have my medication with me. I really hope you'll excuse me. Tell Sarah and the girls I'll see them at work in the morning."

"Okay. You take care of yourself. I'll call and check on you later," Maxie said as she went to Kerra, took her hands, and patted them.

"I'll walk you to your car?" Dustin said.

"That's not necessary. You need to get back to your son and his party. And by the way, he is an absolutely adorable little boy, so smart and well mannered. I know you're proud."

"Yes, he's very special. And thank you for the compliment to him. He seems to have taken quite a liking to you."

"And I to him. He's a bit irresistible. Please tell him I'm sorry I had to leave. Maxie, maybe you can bring him by the dental office to see me."

"I'll do that," Maxie said. "Now, *I'm* going to walk you to your car. And if you need anything after you get home, please call me."

Dustin walked outside, pulled a bottle of water from the cooler and sat down on a bench near the swimming pool.

"Hey Brites, what's up?" Jason asked while sitting down next to Dustin. "Your mind seems to be someplace else since you saw Kerra."

Dustin lifted a bottle of water to his lips and swallowed a drink.

"It was just kind of a shock. We've actually run into one another twice at the beach and spoke briefly. We never exchanged names. And I didn't know if she was a tourist or a local. I had no idea she was the girl Mom kept telling me was new at Doctor Smith's office."

Jason lifted his beer bottle and took a drink. "Yeah, small world isn't it?" He was contemplating whether he should tell Dustin that Kerra was the girl he met for dinner two weeks before. Then he decided there was no need. Dustin wasn't interested in a relationship with anyone, or so he said. But the way he looked at Kerra and the silence that came over him after she and Shay walked away was a sign of something Jason had not observed before in his partner.

"Okay, food's up! Everyone out of the pool!" Hugh Brites called out.

Kids and parents left the pool and wrapped towels around themselves before going into the sunroom to eat. Sarah, Lois and Vicki had helped Maxie put the burgers and hot dogs in the buns and place them on trays for the guests.

"Has anyone seen Kerra?" Sarah asked.

Maxie explained about the headache and gave the girls the message that Kerra would see them at work the next morning.

After the meal, Dustin came from the kitchen with the sheet cake. He lit six candles. "Five for the birthday, and one to grow on," he said. Shay blew out the candles with one breath. Everyone yelled and clapped for him.

"Okay, okay! Thank you!" Shay said like a little man. Then standing on the bench to the picnic table he made an announcement.

"Before Gammie can cut the cake, and because it's my birthday, everyone has to hear a joke."

Everyone's eyes and smiling faces were glued to Shay.

"Okay, when do you go on red and stop on green?" he asked.

We don't know, everyone said in unison. "When do you go on red and stop on green?"

"When you're eating a watermelon!" Shay shouted.

Everyone laughed. Most everyone knew that Hugh was the one responsible for teaching Shay the innocent jokes to create fun and laughs. Learning to do this had given the youngster an ability to get Dustin to sometimes laugh when no one else could.

After the joke, Maxie cut the cake and Shay began opening his gifts. In all the fun and crowded room, he had not realized that

Kerra was gone. When he opened the card that she had left for him, he recognized the letters that spelled her name, and held up the twenty dollar bill.

"Money for my savings account," he squealed. "Miss Kerra, thank you." He looked around for her or to hear her voice.

"Miss Kerra had to go home, Honey," Maxie said. "She had a headache. But she'll see you again."

"Can we call her?" Shay asked. "Maybe later. Right now you have other friends to thank for coming to your party and for the gifts they brought to you."

Shay's attention returned to opening more birthday presents while the other children created a perimeter around him to see and inspect each item. Dustin put wrapping paper and discarded paper plates in a trash bag. In the back of his mind he knew that Kerra had left not because of a headache, but for some other reason that he had spotted in her demeanor.

After everyone said their good-byes and departed from the Brites' home, Dustin helped Maxie clean up and put away the remaining food. He was searching for a way to open a conversation with his mom about Kerra, but with no idea how, he just began.

"Mom, are you and Shay up to something?"

"What do you mean? About what?"

"You know. This girl, Kerra."

"I wouldn't exactly refer to her as a *girl*," Maxie said as she wiped off the counter top. "She's a very attractive *woman* and has a good heart."

"No doubt she's attractive. But I don't think you've known her long enough to know how good of a heart she has. It takes time to really know someone."

"Well then," Maxie said almost belligerently, "Why don't *you* take the time to *learn*!? Dustin, I love you and as your mother, I want nothing but the best for you. It would be easy for me to be selfish and want to keep you and Shay under my wing and total care for the rest of my natural life, but that's not right. You can't keep finding reasons to not give love and a home of your own a chance. It's not fair to you or Shay. I won't always be around, you know."

Dustin threw down the dish towel that he had in his hands.

"Mom, I mean no disrespect and I love you. But please stop trying to make me do something I don't want to. I have no room left in me for potential disappointments. I've seen too much with the men and women I served with. First we grew up too fast seeing what no one should on battlefields. Then the battles I know that my friends have fought to keep relationships after they returned home. Too many down the tubes and letting themselves fall further into the pit. It's best I raise Shay alone rather than end up in a relationship that may not last."

"So, because of your own personal fears about something that you don't even know for sure could be reality or not, you're willing to shortchange Shay."

"Mom, I'm protecting Shay. I don't want to start dating someone that Shay might like just to have his heart broken if it didn't work out. This isn't just about me!"

Hugh came downstairs from Shay's room. "What's going on you two?"

"Nothing," both Dustin and Maxie said in unison.

"Oh, another mother and son disagreement?" Hugh asked.

"Guess you could say that," said Maxie.

Dustin remained silent as he moved the broom around the kitchen floor.

"Well," said Hugh, "if it's about the same argument, Max, you need to leave the boy alone. When he least expects it he's gonna be hit in the head or should I say heart with love like a ton of bricks.

What Dustin didn't want anyone to know, not even his own heart, was that bricks were already tumbling. The question was how to stop it.

Back at the cottage Kerra took two Tylenol and lay down on the bed. Kitten curled up next to her.

"Well," Kerra said as she stroked the purring cat, "This was supposed to have been a good day, but it seems I got a few surprises I never expected."

With the sound of the surf wafting through the open bedroom window, Kerra closed her eyes, relaxed and drifted to sleep.

CHAPTER NINE

"How are you feeling this morning?" Sarah asked when Kerra arrived at work on Monday.

"Much better. Thank you. How was the rest of the party? I was so sorry I couldn't stay."

"Shay certainly missed you when he opened the gift you left for him. He was looking all over for you. I think that little boy has a special feeling for you. Maxie will probably be bringing him by to say thank you."

"They're a wonderful family. Shay introduced me to his dad, Dustin, yesterday. Is this the Dustin you girls were saying was the most eligible hunk and war hero in town?"

"Yes it is," Sarah said with a grin as she tapped the pencil in her hand against her desk.

"The introduction was a bit embarrassing for me."

"Why?"

"Well, Jason was standing next to Dustin. Jason and I have met for dinner. I turned him down about going to a party over the weekend. It must have been Shay's party. And I've actually met Dustin in passing on the beach."

"Oh my gosh! When, how?"

"It was by a near accident. He was coming out of the water with his kayak. My beach umbrella flew out of the sand and almost smacked him against the head. It was the pinnacle of my most embarrassing moments. Then on another day he spoke briefly after paddle boarding. We didn't really have a conversation or anything."

Kerra remembered exactly why Dustin had spoken. It was the day he thought she was having a panic attack after her dream about Winston. But she wasn't going into that with Sarah.

"We didn't even exchange names. So, when Shay introduced me yesterday, and then I learn Shay's mom is deceased, everything became a bit more than I could process. The headache came on and I had to go home."

"Don't worry about it," said Sarah. "First of all, turning Jason down was what he needed. I think it's especially funny because the irony is that although you didn't know what party he was inviting you to, you turned him down for a five year old! That should put his ego a little on edge! Second, the story about Shay's mom is local knowledge. Nothing bad. Just a story of sad circumstances. Ask Maxie sometime. She'll tell you all about it. And as for Dustin, well, he suffered a lot in the wars. He's a wonderful man, but very guarded. He doesn't seem to want to have a relationship with anyone but his immediate family."

Kerra understood being guarded. Sarah's description of Dustin was how she would pretty much describe herself.

"Thanks for the insight," Kerra told Sarah. "It helps."

After being at the station for a few hours, Jason finally attempted a conversation with Dustin.

"Hey, Buddy, you're quiet this morning. What's going on?"

"Nothing. Just reviewing some information for an ocean safety training class I'm presenting today at the middle school."

As Jason turned to walk to the back of the fire station, Dustin called to him.

"Jason, could I ask you a question?"

Jason turned back around. "Sure, man. Go."

"Is Kerra the girl you told me about a couple of weeks ago? The one you said was playing hard to get?"

Jason hesitated a moment before speaking.

"Yes, she is. Why?"

"Are you planning on asking her out again?"

"Actually, Dus, I don't think she's interested in me for anymore than an acquaintance."

"What makes you say that?"

"Man, I can tell. There was something going on in just the way you two looked at each other yesterday. Why don't you ask her out?"

"I don't know. Maybe. Shay and Mom sure seem to like her. I don't even know if I'd know how to date again. What to say. What to do. I'm a combat veteran, a dad, a fire and rescue crew member, a swimmer, and a son. Don't know how good of company I'd be on a date. I'm not the player you are, Dude."

Jason laughed. "I'm sure if it's the right woman, everything will come natural."

"Is there anything you can tell me about her?" Dustin asked as he rose from the chair where he sat and went to the coffee pot.

"I'll just tell you that she's a transplant from Wisconsin and the daughter of a dairy farmer. She has a good sense of humor, loves the outdoors, and she's a very independent woman. You're on your own to learn anything else. All else I'll say is that I don't think you should let her get away without trying. I'll see you later."

Jason turned and walked away as Dustin sighed in deep thought. "Maybe if I run into her at the beach again, I'll talk to her. Maybe."

When Maxi called the dental office at 9 a.m. to check on Kerra, Sarah confirmed that Kerra had made it to work and was feeling fine. "I'll have her give you a call," Sarah told Maxie, "I know she will appreciate that you checked in on her."

Maxie thanked Sarah and then called Shay to come to the family room where they always sat together for their morning reading time. Maxie had been reading to Shay since he was born, just as she had with Dustin and his sister. She had always believed in the importance of spending time cuddling with her children and one grandchild to create that sense of feeling loved and having fun through reading and learning sounds and words. Shay could already identify the alphabet in both upper and lower case and knew many words by sight. He could also write his name and simple words. For this morning's exercise Maxie found a short story book to read out loud to Shay. Afterwards he began repeating the story back to her in his own words. But before Shay got too far along, he stopped and looked at Maxie.

"Do you think Daddy liked Miss Kerra?"

Maxie smiled at her grandson, his eyes a reflection of his mother's.

"Oh Sweetheart, I'm sure he did. But remember, it was the first time they met."

"Can we invite her for dinner on a night that dad's at home?"

"We'll see. But for now, what do you say about finishing your lesson. Then you can play one of your computer games while I do some house work?"

Shay released a sigh. "Okay," he said. Then turned the page of his book, pointed to the colorful pictures and told Maxie what the characters were doing.

A few minutes after noon Maxie answered her phone.

"Hi Maxie, it's Kerra. Sarah gave me your message. I appreciate your call this morning. I'm doing much better."

"That's good to hear. You had me a bit worried."

"I'm sorry. I have a history of migraines. So sometimes one will attack when I least expect it. After I took my medicine and had a nap, I was good for work this morning."

"I certainly understand," Maxie replied. "After Dustin's military service he dealt with headaches that thank goodness are pretty much under control now."

Before she knew it, Shay was standing beside Maxie. "Gammie, who's on the phone?"

Maxie smiled down at her grandson then spoke again into the receiver.

"Kerra, I have someone I think would like to speak to you."

Shay's eyes and smile grew large. He took the phone receiver from Maxie's hand and placed it against his ear.

"Miss Kerra, is that you?

"Yes it is, Shay. How are you today?"

"I'm doing okay. Thank you for coming to my birthday party and for the birthday money.

"You're welcome, Shay. I bet you got lots of neat gifts."

"I did. But yours was the best. I'm going to put part of it in my bank account."

"That's great. Are you saving for something special?"

"I don't know yet. But Daddy and Gammie tell me saving is good."

"Well, they're right. You have a very wise dad and gammie."

"Gammie says I need to let you get back to work. I'm handing her the phone."

Before Kerra could say goodbye, Maxie was speaking.

"Kerra, thanks for returning my call. I'm glad you're feeling better."

"Thank you," Kerra replied.

"Kerra, one more thing before you go. I was wondering if you'd like to come to the house on Wednesday and have lunch with Shay and me?"

Kerra knew she would have to drive her car from the cottage to work and then to Maxie's. Then she wondered if Dustin would be there. Before she spoke Maxie said, "Dustin and Hugh will both be at work. No one will be here except me and Shay."

"That sounds nice," Kerra said. "I'll see you on Wednesday, shortly after twelve noon."

"Wonderful!" Maxie responded happily. "We'll see you then."

After work and on her way to the cottage, Kerra strolled past the fire and rescue station. None of the crew members were in sight. For this she was grateful since she didn't want to feel awkward again in the presence of both Dustin and Jason. But what she didn't know was that Dustin was standing in a place where he could see her, although she couldn't see him. He took a deep breath and was going to call her name and talk for a minute, but he couldn't. He simply watched Kerra keep walking as she pulled her cell phone from her uniform pocket and placed it against her ear.

Kerra spoke with her mom for a few minutes as she finished her walk to the cottage.

"No news is good news, Mom. All is still well with me. Did the kid's receive the post cards I sent?"

"They sure did. And want to come to the beach. They also saw the photos you put on your facebook page."

"Yeah, I see their notes. And Winston? How's he doing?"

"Winston is doing well. You should call and talk to him. He and his family have no bad feelings against you for moving away. Winston is showing improvement. He actually took a few steps this morning at physical therapy. His mom was so excited when she called. Remember after all this happened, the doctor told Winston and his parents that the recovery window was about two years. Winston hasn't given up and you know he never will. So put a smile on."

"Mom, this is such wonderful news. I promise I'll give him a call and congratulate him."

"That would be awesome, Honey."

After Kerra and her mom said their good-byes, she unlocked and pushed open the cottage door. Kitten galloped softly toward her as she placed her keys, cell phone and lunch bag on the kitchen counter.

"Hello my little companion. It's been a good day for me, how about you?"

Kitten meowed as always in response to Kerra's question.

Kerra was happy that Kitten had come into her life. For as far back in her life as she could remember she had talked to and helped tend all kinds of animals back home at the dairy farm. Her horse named Joe, the cows, calves, chickens, the family dogs and cats that all had names she had helped choose. As she grew older on the farm she had helped mother cows give birth to their calves and learned to recognize when an udder was infected or cancerous and perform the procedure required to block it from the good udders. She could as well have gone to veterinarian school, but chose not to because an animal couldn't tell anyone if they were feeling pain or not. Her heart was just too tender to spend the rest of her days being concerned about others' special pets and animals, although she appreciated all that she had learned and carried all the treasured memories gained as the daughter of a dairy farmer.

Kerra picked up Kitten for a quick cuddle and rub. "I think I'll change, pour a glass of wine, and go outside to wait for the sunset," she said. After returning Kitten to the floor, Kerra pulled a pair of athletic shorts and a sports top from a drawer to replace her uniform. On her way outside with a glass of wine, she picked up the new weekly issue of *Woman's World.*

CHAPTER TEN

Maxie loved history. She always told her children and now her grandson the story of the community where they were born and raised. For Shay, just as she did for Dustin and his sister, she made every attempt to keep them interested in learning, even with sock puppets. She had told them about how the white sand beaches of Panama City were of no use to people of the 1800's. Only Old Town St Andrew, the name given by Spanish conquistadors along St Andrew's Bay, and fifteen miles from their house, held value because it was fertile land for harvesting crops. During the Civil War, Old Town St Andrew was destroyed, but after the war, it began to grow again and survive because of the abundance of fish in the surrounding waters. Other communities and businesses grew inland around the bays and peninsulas. Bridges were built to connect communities separated by bodies of water. Civil War veterans created a retirement community and built homes and gardens for themselves in the area now known as Lynn Haven where, back then, one dollar purchased an acre of land. But the name Panama City didn't exist until 1905 when the United Fruit Company relocated from New Orleans to the St Andrews port. From here, United Fruit could easily reach Panama City, Panama. Community leaders, pleased that the new company had brought jobs, named the unincorporated area Panama City. Even the founder of Coca-Cola jumped on board and helped with funding to complete the railway in 1908. But the masses continued to say that there was no use or future for 'ugly white sand'. Then developer Gideon Thomas arrived in 1935 with his vision of a resort town. A piece of white-sand property sold for $100 to $600 per lot. Slow and sure, even during the depression, the sugar sand beach area grew, and the *Washington News Daily* stated "Panama City has a destiny as sure as the sun will rise tomorrow..." Now, in the twenty-first century, a small sliver of the sugar sand, especially beach front, would sell for hundreds of thousands, even millions.

The home where Maxie and her family lived on the west end of Panama City Beach had existed there since 1950. At the time it was built, only a small number of beach cottages and middle class homes surrounded it. Except for Miracle Strip Highway, now Front Beach Road, streets and driveways were mostly sand and crushed oyster shells. Anyone could walk with ease down paths cut through the tall grasses and sea oats where the tiny beach mice were now a protected species along with a number of beach nesting birds like the small yellow-billed least terns and the small pale snowy plovers with short beaks. The birds lay their eggs in the sand or sea shells and were often trampled by beach goers. Sea turtles were protected and volunteers helped ensure nesting areas were guarded and that as many hatchlings as possible made it into the gulf waters.

Maxie belonged to a local conservation organization that worked diligently to help protect the animals, birds, and plants indigenous to her community. She and Shay had taken their Wednesday morning walk together on the beach to pick up trash. This she considered one of his educational activities so he could learn the importance of keeping the beaches clean and the dangers of plastic and other trash to sea life. A sea turtle was once found with a plastic grocery bag covering its head. If it had been discovered much later it would have died. But thanks to a call to Gulf World personnel by a passerby, this one was saved.

After their visit to the beach, Maxie and Shay returned home to prepare for lunch. At 12:10 p.m. the door bell rang.

"I'll get it! I'll get it!" Shay yelled as he ran from the kitchen to the front door.

Maxie continued putting placemats and napkins on the dining table.

"Well, hello there!" Kerra said when Shay opened the door. "I think I'm supposed to report here for lunch today."

Shay opened the door wide. "Gammie is fixing chicken salad sandwiches and fruit salad."

"Well that sounds wonderful. I can't wait."

"Shay, invite Miss Kerra in and close the door! You'll let out all the air conditioning!"

Shay took Kerra by the hand as though to help her cross the threshold. Once she was clear of the doorway he closed the door.

Kerra smiled broadly at the five year old. "You are such a little gentleman."

Maxie came to Kerra and offered a hug that Kerra accepted before they walked to the dining table.

"Here, have a seat," Maxie said. "I hope chicken salad with walnuts and grapes and fruit salad is okay with you."

"It's perfect."

Shay crawled into the chair next to Kerra while Maxie put the plates for each of them on the table followed by a glass of ice and bottle of water. After Maxie sat down and before she could say anything, Shay started his own conversation.

"Miss Kerra, where were you born? I was born at the hospital in Panama City."

"I was born in a hospital in the state of Wisconsin.

"Where is Wisconsin?"

"Well, it's a state pretty far from here. If you have a map, I can show you."

"Okay! I have a map of all the states on the wall in my bedroom. Maybe we can look at it after we eat. And I can show you my crab friends that Dad painted for me."

"I don't see why not," Kerra replied. "But let's make sure we eat all this wonderful lunch that Gammie made for us."

Maxie smiled. Watching the interaction between Kerra and Shay made her heart warm. Kerra took a bite of her sandwich while Shay put a piece of fresh watermelon in his mouth.

"You know he will talk to you about anything and everything if you let him," Maxie laughed. "And like a little adult."

"That's perfectly alright," said Kerra. "I have two nephews back in Wisconsin. He helps me not to miss them so much. And besides, from what I've read, an only child who is stimulated by adults the majority of time, is much more mature in their behavior and conversation."

"How old are your nephews?" asked Shay

"They are eight and five."

"Can they visit sometime, and swim in the pool with me?"

"I'm sure they'll visit. I'm just not sure when right now."

"Eat your lunch, Shay. Remember, Miss Kerra has to get back to work, so let her finish eating."

"Yes Ma'am."

Outside the kitchen window a hummingbird lit on the red bloom of the bottle brush plant.

The two women chit chatted while they enjoyed the meal and Shay's sharing a joke with them.

"What's the biggest ant in the world?" asked Shay.

"We don't know," said Maxie and Kerra in unison. "What's the biggest ant in the world?"

"An eleph-ant!" Shay exclaimed!

"You are just too smart, Shay Brites!" Kerra said as she ran her fingers through his hair.

"You have such a beautiful home here," Kerra said as she rose with her plate to place in the sink. "Have you always lived on Panama City Beach?"

"All my life," Maxie replied as she picked up the dishes she and Shay had used. "My husband, too. We've watched the area go through a complete metamorphosis. From a rather quiet area to the hustle and bustle you now see. But it'll quiet down after school starts in August."

Maxie shared a bit of the history of the area with Kerra and how southerners referred to it as their very own *Redneck Riviera*, which of course Kerra found amusing.

"By the way, do you have any plans for July 4th?" Maxie asked.

"I haven't really thought about it."

Shay interjected with vigor. "We have the best fireworks anywhere! We can see them in the sky from our own backyard."

"Really!" Kerra exclaimed. "That must be pretty cool!"

Before anyone said another word, they all looked toward the front door that had just opened.

There stood Dustin.

"Hey, Son. What in the world brings you home in the middle of the day?" Maxie looked puzzled.

Shay ran to his dad and wrapped his arms around his legs.

"Hey Sport, what's going on?"

Kerra was shocked, yet captured by the way Dustin looked in the navy blue shorts and a gray t-shirt. The way his biceps popped just below the shirt sleeve, the veins in his triceps, his broad shoulders, and belted slim waist. Although she had seen him half dressed in a swimsuit, there was also something to be admired about a fit man in any type of uniform.

Shay released his arms from around his dad.

"Gammie invited Miss Kerra for lunch today. She was going to show me on my map where she was born in Wisconsin. And I was going to introduce her to Speedy and Slowpoke. You want to come with us?"

"Buddy, I'd love to, but I have to grab something from my file cabinet and get back to the station."

Dustin gave Kerra a quick hello and smile before he darted toward the home office. Shay took Kerra's hand and led her upstairs to his room. Kerra was glad for the quick escape. Maxie just shook her head and turned to washing dishes.

CHAPTER ELEVEN

Thursday was Dustin's day off. His list of things to do during the day included changing the oil and filter in his truck and his mom's car, taking Shay for a swim lesson, going to the gym, and most importantly going down to the beach later in the evening to see if Kerra was sitting in her usual place. He didn't know that he could ask her out, but he wanted to at least apologize to her for his mother's match making attempts. Although he didn't bring the subject up to his mom, he couldn't believe she had invited Kerra to the house yesterday for lunch. He didn't want Shay to become confused about Kerra's relationship to the family.

By 6:30 p.m. Kerra was sitting in her beach chair with her feet in the water enjoying the breath of the evening breeze. As the sun prepared to set in the West, a gossamer moon was rising in the East. There was no mistaking Dustin when he walked from the water carrying his kayak. Kerra sat up in her chair and waved. Dustin waved back as he strolled in her direction, which surprised Kerra. When he reached her, he placed his kayak on the sand and sat down on the front tip of it, then leaned forward with his elbows propped on his knees.

"How was the water and kayaking?" Kerra asked, trying to open a conversation.

"Doesn't get much better than this," Dustin said as he straightened his back and looked out over the calm gulf. "We've been lucky to have so many days of good beach weather. We could be due a tropical storm anytime. And hurricane season is already here."

"I suppose I should keep an eye close to the weather channel."

"It never hurts. And don't forget to put your hurricane survival kit together."

"Yes sir. I have no doubt that following your instructions will be most helpful. After all, your umbrella instruction proved to be right on."

Dustin exhibited a slight laugh. "So I take it that no other beach goers have met your flying umbrella."

"Nope. It's been sand tight."

For a brief moment, neither of them spoke until Dustin decided to bring up the subject that had been on his mind all day.

"Kerra, I'm a bit embarrassed. I just want to apologize for my mom." Dustin picked up a sea shell from the sand between his feet and looked at it. It was whole, the size of a quarter, white and brown.

"Why would you say that?" Kerra was puzzled.

"Haven't you figured her out? She's trying to play match maker. And Shay is just as bad. And I don't want either of them disappointed. For some reason they are dead set on the idea that I need a girlfriend, or wife, an addition to the family that doesn't exist."

Kerra leaned back in her chair with her arms resting on the chair's arm rests and gave him a steady look as he raked his fingers through the sand as though looking for something.

"But you aren't interested in any of that?" Kerra questioned cautiously.

"Oh, no. I've offended you. Haven't I? Please let me explain." Dustin took a deep breath, looked up at the sky and then brought his gaze back to Kerra.

Before Kerra could speak, he continued.

"Listen, I don't know how much my mom has told you about me, but I just don't consider myself boyfriend or husband material. I don't want her trying to get someone interested in me when I know I can't return the feeling. I want you to know that you are a very sweet, attractive woman. Shay and Mom adore you. So I must really be messed up to not want to ask you out on a date."

"So, why do you believe you're so messed up?"

"I don't know that I can give you details. All I can tell you is that I'm a combat veteran with several tours to the sand box under my belt. I watched some of my buddies die, children suffer and so many other things that I guess I've locked myself down. I don't have it in me to give any more of myself away, or bring anyone else into my issues that sometimes raise their ugly heads."

"What do you mean by that?" asked Kerra. Suddenly she was seeing part of herself in what Dustin was saying. Since the car accident she hadn't wanted her life to extend much further than day to day existence, much as she had seen with Winston who was caught in his paralysis and therapy.

Dustin shifted his feet in the sand and threw a piece of a broken sand dollar toward the water.

"Oh, I'm sure you know what I'm talking about, whether you understand it or not. After surviving in war, the more people you come to like or love leaves the possibility of more pain just waiting to happen that I don't want. For those you love and watch die or become debilitated, you carry guilt for still living or for having all your limbs, or even a mind that still functions. And there's always a dream that's going to creep in and leave the bed sheets soaked with sweat while I try to remember if I'm here at home or back on a battlefield. So there, you have my story. As much as I can tell you anyway. Mom means well. But she doesn't understand why I feel the way I do. I just can't create a deep relationship with anyone other than those that were already in my life before the other me that I've become."

"But wasn't your dad a Vietnam veteran?"

"Yes, he was. And Mom dealt with a lot after they married. And she's been by my side since I returned home and left the military. A mom doesn't mind changing sweat filled sheets or listening during the night as though you're still a child to stop you from sleep walking before you hurt yourself or someone else. A mom doesn't mind calling your name from another side of a room in hopes you wake up before you believe she's an enemy. I'm much better. But my mom and dad are used to these things in case something happened that caused me to go backwards instead of continuing to move forward. And I work with guys that know what to do if something crazy happened on the job. But I can't see even stepping through the door of looking for a relationship when I know the statistics of failed relationships and marriages, especially with combat veterans."

"Dustin," Kerra said gently, "I know I can't even begin to imagine what you have been through. But, I do understand to some degree exactly what you mean about guilt and locking down. My best friend back in Wisconsin is paralyzed from the waist down. I was driving the car the night of the accident that put him in a wheelchair, maybe for life. The accident wasn't even my fault, but to know I can walk and carry on a normal life and Winston can't still haunts me. After I got out of the hospital with my own bumps and bruises, I worked with a therapist to try and get a grip. I know what happened that night when we were broadsided was totally out of my control. But then came all the questions of why?"

"I know that one well," Dustin said. "Had a bit of my own therapy to try and balance all that stuff. All I know now is that I have to keep my eyes on one day at a time. Focus to do what I can to make a difference where I'm supposed to. Save a life when I'm supposed to. I tend to believe now that everything is owned by destiny."

"I guess," said Kerra. "Have you heard the saying that if you want to make God laugh just tell him your plan?"

"Yep, that's one of Mom's favorites," Dustin laughed. "Mom has a quote for everything. Her favorite for me these days is 'You're confined only by the walls you build around yourself.' Maybe she's right."

"Can I ask you something rather personal? If you don't want to answer, I understand and no problem," Kerra said.

"Go ahead. I haven't talked this much at one time to anyone in a very long time. What's the question?"

"It's about Shay. What happened to his mom?"

Dustin hesitated a moment, searching for where to begin.

"Shay's mom died in a car accident here on the beach. She was a wonderful gal. We went to school together our entire life. We were more like best friends. Not really girlfriend – boyfriend. She was a swimmer like me. My girlfriend broke up with me after my first deployment to the sand box. She said she knew then that she wasn't military girlfriend or wife material. She couldn't deal with the waiting, no daily or weekly phone calls. She needed someone she could see every day. I had signed a six year contract with the Army.

I loved being in the military. But with my job, I was in and out of the sand box every so many months. After the second deployment and seeing buddies die and injured both times, I didn't want to die without leaving a part of myself behind. I didn't want my folks not to have a part of me with them if something happened, and at the time I knew my chances of being taken out by an explosive device or enemy fire was as good as anyone's.

I was home before leaving on my third deployment. Shay's mom and I were spending time together talking about old times, fun times, times before 9/11. She's the only person I ever told just how scarred I was at times. And that I didn't believe I'd return. I asked her if she would consider carrying my child so a part of me would be left for my folks who she loved and adored as much as they did her. We talked about there being no guarantee that she would get pregnant. But two months after that encounter, and before I deployed again, she called me with the news. We were both ecstatic. She was six months along when I deployed again. If I returned, we would each share time with Shay and I would provide for him. In the event I didn't return, I created a will and trust for my life insurance to go to for Shay's future with Mom and Dad as executors. I first saw Shay when he was two months old, and I had two more years on my contract. I was back in the states at Fort Benning, Georgia, when I received the news that her car had been broadsided by a drunk driver on Front Beach Road. Shay was only six months old and was with my mom when the accident happened."

"Dustin, I just don't know what to say. You have been through so much."

"Goes back to destiny, I guess. War zone or your own backyard, when it's someone's time to go from here, it's time. Shay's maternal grandparents eventually moved from the area because they couldn't bear to see the crash site every time they went out driving. So, my mom and dad took care of my son until I separated from the Army when Shay was two. Then when I came home permanently, they still had to take care of him while helping me through VA red tape, doctor and therapists appointments, and making sure I didn't over medicate with all the prescription drugs the VA hands out like band aids. If it weren't for their support and not giving up, I'd be another casualty of war and the VA system, and a very dysfunctional parent and part of society. Of course after some time passed, Mom would give me a good kick in the seat, metaphorically I mean, when I began feeling sorry for myself. She always reminded me what Dad overcame, and his dad before him as a World War II prisoner of war. Dad always reminded me of my swimming and how it had been my love before the military. I eventually had to take responsibility for my own mind, body, and spirit and kick it into gear. So, there you have it, plus more. And here I sit today functioning as best I can as the proud dad of a great son."

"So, how often does Shay see his mom's parents?"

"We visit them in South Florida when I take vacation. When he's older, if they would like for him to come alone and visit for a longer time in summer, we'll make it happen as long as Shay's happy with it."

"Dustin, I just want you to know that I adore that little boy of yours and your mom. I hope you won't mind if I stay friends with them. Maxie is precious and has become like another mom, even if she has been trying to be a match maker. Of course that never crossed my mind. But if you believe that's what she's trying to do, she's no different from my mom. I wasn't here a month when she asked me if I'd met any eligible bachelors."

"Really. What did you tell her?"

"I told her I wasn't interested in meeting any eligible bachelors. I needed to meet some personal goals before I thought about meeting anyone to settle with in a relationship."

With all the conversation, Kerra and Dustin both were now more relaxed. Dustin felt better knowing that this woman wasn't looking for a relationship. And now Kerra knew his story and was clear about him. But on the other hand, both of them still felt an electrical current when they were near one another.

"So what are your goals?" Dustin asked.

"I've made my first one."

"What's that?"

"I left Wisconsin and moved to the most beautiful beaches in the world."

"And what brought that on," asked Dustin. By now he had moved from sitting on his kayak to sitting cross legged in the sand and raking it into a pile for a sand castle.

"As I tell everyone, Wisconsin winters are so cold with winds so hard it takes a half dozen people to open a barn door. The snow is relentless. I was so depressed after the car accident that my mom and I looked for a warm sunny place to visit and see if it would help me. I had read that air around a beach has these mood-lifting negative ions that help spark happy hormones in the brain! And I sure needed some happy sparks!"

"Well, is it true?"

"What?" asked Kerra.

"Do you feel happier here?"

"I do. I really do. And your mom and Shay have added to that." Kerra was now sitting in the sand and pushing it toward the castle that Dustin was creating.

"What other goals are on your list?"

"I want to take my mom on a Mediterranean Cruise. Since I've been here, I've been thinking about learning to kayak and paddle board. Which by the way, can you recommend where I might go for lessons?"

"Mmmm, let me think," said Dustin..

"I think I know someone very qualified to teach you."

"Really? Will I have to drive to a location far from here?"

"No Ma'am, I can teach you right here."

Kerra hesitated a moment. "Are you for real? You'll teach me?"

"Sure. Are you available Saturday?"

"Just tell me what time."

"9:00 a.m.?"

"Deal."

By now the sun had slid into the gulf, leaving dusk to ease into night. With beach chair in hand, Kerra walked with Dustin to the shower at the board walk.

Kerra was taking in the movement of his muscles as he shifted here and there to rinse his kayak. She watched as he lifted up his face for the water to flow down his eyes, the tip of his nose, chin and the rest of his body. She was almost in a daze when Dustin turned off the water and spoke.

"I'm assuming you live in walking distance from here."

"Ahhh, yep. Just down the way at the cottage next to the beach front two-story."

"Let me walk with you. I think it's getting a little dark for you to walk alone."

"You don't have to," Kerra said. "There are plenty of street lights."

"But, I wouldn't be doing my civic duty if I didn't walk a lady who is alone to her nearby home. It's getting late and it would add to my traumatic experiences if something happened. Never take anything for granted. Just because there are street lights and you live nearby doesn't make the street 100% safe." Dustin took her by the elbow and turned her in the direction of the cottage.

"Believe me," Kerra said, "I never take anything for granted."

"Mmmm, seems we have a common philosophy," Dustin replied.

"Seems so," Kerra said as they reached the door of the cottage. "I enjoyed our talk. Thank you for sharing things with me that I know must be very difficult. And I look forward to my kayak lesson on Saturday."

"Me, too. See you then."

The two hesitated and looked in each other's eyes for a brief moment. Dustin wanted to give Kerra a quick kiss, like an old friend. But he decided not to and stepped back. The feelings inside his body were beginning to run amuck. He couldn't take any chance that he would break his own rule or offend Kerra since she wasn't looking for more than a friendship.

Only after Kerra turned, unlocked her door and disappeared inside the cottage did Dustin return to his truck and head for home with thoughts about Kerra that he didn't want to admit. And little did he know the same thoughts were with her.

CHAPTER TWELVE

Before Kerra showered, she pressed the phone number for Winston's home. It was time she spoke with him and stopped feeling sorry for herself. She had created her own burdens. Deep down she knew that Winston would never want her to limit her personal happiness because he was learning to live differently. And after listening to Dustin's stories she had gained a new perspective. She had been so wrapped up in her own experience and thoughts that she couldn't unravel the ropes of guilt to free herself.

The phone rang three times in Wisconsin before Winston's mom answered.

"Hi, Mrs. Summers, this is Kerra. I hope it's not too late for my call."

"Kerra! What a surprise! It's so wonderful to hear from you. Your mom tells us that the Florida sunshine is doing wonders for you."

"I believe it is. It's a great place. Maybe you and Mr. Summers can bring Winston to visit sometime. I think the sun, sand, and beach would do wonders for him."

"That's definitely something we will consider. Did you hear that Winston took his first step in therapy today?"

"That's why I'm calling. Mom called and told me. I wanted to congratulate Winston. Is this a good time?"

"It's perfect. My husband was just about to help Winston get settled for the evening. I know that he'll have a really good night after hearing your voice. Let me take the phone to him."

She didn't know why butterflies were flittering in her stomach. Maybe because she had not spoken to Winston in the months she'd been in Florida. She had sent facebook notes and postcards, but that was never as good as the voice of a person that was supposed to be your best friend.

"Kerra! It's about time you called! I've missed your voice, girl!" Winston was ecstatic.

Kerra smiled and her stomach settled. "Hey you! I heard you proved doctors wrong today!"

"You know I'm not going to let this wheel chair stay tied to my butt. I told you that from the beginning. And if for some reason it was, you know I won't let it stop me from still being a dairy farmer. Dad got me another truck and had hand controls installed. I get myself down to see your dad to keep up with what's going on. And I'm building up some pretty good upper body strength with therapy and weights."

"I'm just so proud of you." Kerra wiped away tears that were sliding down her cheeks. "I didn't even know you had gone down to the dairy."

"I told your folks not to tell you. I figured when you decided to call I'd be able to tell you everything myself. You know Kerra, you've always allowed unnecessary guilt and depression to rule you since the accident. It wasn't your fault and you sure could never have made my injuries any better by doing that to yourself. And just so you'll know, I recently received a letter from the family of the person that ran the red light that night. I think your mom has one addressed to you, too. They are apologizing for their elderly mom who caused the accident and died later while in a coma. She wasn't supposed to be driving due to her health issues. Other than what their insurance company has paid out, they wanted to know if there is anything else they can do. Kerra, so many were affected by this accident, but we are still here. And we're going to keep on dreaming. So, girl, '*Don't Worry, Be Happy!*'" Winston sang.

"Oh my best friend Winston, we should have had this talk a long time ago!"

"I tried but you wouldn't listen. Now, tell me about that beach town where you're living."

Kerra told Winston about the cottage, Kitten, the sunsets, her new friends at work, and her second mom, Maxie. Before she knew it, they had talked and laughed for an hour. After the call ended, she had a sense of peace that she had not felt in two years.

"Hurricane season in Florida began June 1 and ends November 30," stated the woman on the local weather channel. "Although things currently look calm for the season, know the difference between a hurricane watch and a hurricane warning. A watch means that conditions are right within 36 hours for a hurricane and you should begin making preparations. A warning means a 24 hour window for a hurricane and your preparations should be complete, along with knowing the evacuation route. Always be prepared with your disaster supplies kit and first aid kit. For more information please contact your local Red Cross office in Bay County or go online to the National Hurricane Center website."

Kerra turned off the television in preparation to leave for work. She had slept well the night before and felt refreshed after the talk with Winston. She hummed 'Don't Worry, Be Happy' as she gathered her keys and lunch bag. It was Friday, a little overcast, but reported to be a clear weekend. Although there were days when large bundles of clouds gathered and exhaled rolls of thunder and streaks of lightening with only a drop or two of rain in one place while producing a quick heavy rain elsewhere. Tropical storms out in the gulf brought in heavy rain and strong winds from thirty-nine to seventy-three miles per hour that whipped palm fronds sideways and created high heavy surf that dared experienced surfers.

Kerra decided to drive the short distance to the office just in case the morning dark clouds decided to remain throughout the day and drop rain later in the evening. As she passed the fire and rescue station, she thought about Dustin and how comfortable their time together talking had been. Actually, too comfortable. She had never found herself so at ease other than with Winston. And there was one more difference. Whereas she had never had a sexual interest for Winston, the sexual attraction ran pretty strong when she was near Dustin. But she and Dustin both had been clear with one another that they were not at a place in life for a romantic relationship. And now she wasn't too sure about the kayak lesson with him. Maybe spending time together on Saturday would be too much.

"He's probably rethinking his offer anyway," she thought. "I'll just call and tell him that I forgot about something I already had scheduled. The worst he can think is that I'm a flake."

The Friday work day passed quickly. Kerra took Sarah up on a Friday evening stroll through Pier Park located across from the beach and city pier. They could choose from any number of restaurants for dinner and wander in and out of a great number of shops loaded with beach clothing, t-shirts for tourists, jewelry, trinkets and beach wall art for every personality. Sarah found a small canvas for her apartment that read, 'You're never fully dressed unless you're wearing flip flops.' Kerra selected one with painted flip flops and beach sand to mail to Winston that read, 'You're the flip in my flop.'

After exploring many of the shops, the women selected Margaritaville for dinner. The restaurant sat across the street from the beach and offered a perfect view of the sunset. They decided on sharing nachos. The dish large enough for more than two was stacked with chips, cheese, chili, guacamole and sour cream. Happy Hour provided a buy one, get one free margarita. Recorded Jimmy Buffet songs played in between sets of live entertainment. A girl on stilts and dressed in bright colored Caribbean style clothing strolled from table to table. She blew up balloons and twisted them into animal shapes for children or created twisted balloons that became head ornaments for children or adults.

"What are you doing for July 4th?" Sarah asked.

"You're the second person to ask me that," Kerra said. "Maxie asked me the last time I talked with her. Is there a big celebration around here?"

"Pretty nice. Fireworks are set off from barges at the end of the city and county piers and at the harbor across the bridge in Panama City. People buy packages of fireworks and keep the miles of beach lit up for hours as far as you can see. Maxie usually invites people to her house for a cookout. There's a great view of the fireworks from Maxie's back yard."

"That's what Shay told me. Sounds like fun."

The girls took a sip of their blended margaritas.

"So," Sarah said, "Have you talked to Maxie this week and learned about Shay's mom?"

"No. But you'll be surprised that Dustin and I had a long conversation last night. We ran into each other at the beach. He told me he wanted to apologize for his mom's attempts to play match maker. One thing led to another and we were sharing stories, so I got the whole scoop directly from Dustin."

Sarah couldn't believe what she was hearing.

"Girl, you've got to be kidding!"

"No, not at all. By the time we finished talking, we had almost built an entire sand castle together."

"Ooooh! Maybe that's a symbol of something yet to be!" Sarah said with wide eyes.

"Oh, no, girl. I'm not interested and Dustin isn't either in a relationship like that. We were both clear with each other. We share some common philosophies. He actually offered to give me kayak lessons starting tomorrow. But I'm calling to change that plan for now."

"Why? Are you crazy? Do you know how many women around here would give their eye teeth to spend that time with him?"

"Oh, I suppose I could make a guess, but maybe that's why he steers clear of women. Because he doesn't want to give the wrong impression or mislead anyone."

"Maybe. I just wonder what made him open up to you."

"Maybe because I don't give off vibes of needing or wanting a romantic relationship."

"Maybe," replied Sarah.

"I have a question for you," said Kerra. "Do you know if Maxie has a habit of trying to play match maker?"

"Can't say I know of her doing it. We're friends and she's never mentioned anyone to me. But I can tell you that she did ask me, Lois and Vicki what we thought about you. Of course we gave you all thumbs up. I think she sees something very special in you. Something she's trusting is so special that she sees you as a good person to be in her son and grandson's life."

"But why not you?" asked Kerra.

"Because Maxie knows I've always had a thing for Jason from the time we were in junior high together."

"Oh, got it."

The waiter brought the huge order of nachos.

Kerra looked at the time on her cell phone. It was already 9:00 p.m. She bit her bottom lip as she second guessed calling Dustin and cancelling the kayak lesson.

Dustin spent Friday at work thinking about how easy it had been to talk to Kerra. She was different. Not the flirty swing her hair around type. Confident but not sassy and most of all honest. Now he was beginning to argue with both his heart and head. Were these the attributes his mom had recognized and put her on a match making mission? And although he had set a boundary for himself not to have a romantic interest, he was still a man who could lust, and he didn't want lust to drive him beyond his personal boundary. And that could be easy to do when he thought about Kerra. He was no longer sure he should be her kayak instructor. And secondly, if his mother knew, she would begin asking too many questions and so would Jason and everyone else. What was he thinking last night when he offered to teach her? He would have to find a reason to cancel. Something that would keep Kerra from believing he was a complete jerk. But then he remembered he never got her phone number. And he sure wasn't going to call his mom for it. That would surely get the questions rolling. The next best thing would be to leave a note on her door on Saturday morning with a bogus excuse. That would work. Dustin felt relieved.

Just as he was about to write the note the fire department phone rang.

"Station One Fire and Beach Rescue, Dustin Brites here."

Kerra hesitated a moment.

"Hello." Dustin said.

"Hi Dustin. It's me, Kerra."

"Oh, hi there." Dustin suddenly felt trapped. Kerra must be calling to confirm the kayak lesson. Now it wasn't going to be so easy to be a jerk.

"Dustin, I hope you won't think badly of me, but I've got to cancel my lesson with you in the morning. I totally forgot about a prior appointment I had scheduled. Maybe another time?"

"Oh, no problem," Dustin replied with relief. "I understand. I actually have a number of things to do. We'll make it happen later."

"Sure, that sounds good. Enjoy your day off tomorrow. Tell your family hello for me."

"Sure thing," Dustin replied. "You take care. Good night."

"Good night." Kerra sighed with relief as Sarah watched.

"You are crazy girl. I don't know why you cancelled that, but you are C-R-A-Z-Y!"

"It's not just about Dustin," Kerra said as she turned the glass of water in circles that sat in front of her. "I've sort of built a wall around myself that I haven't broken through completely." Kerra spent the next hour telling Sarah about the car accident.

CHAPTER THIRTEEN

July 4th offered a cost free evening of patriotic music performed by the Panama City Symphony Orchestra at Aaron Bessant Park across from the beach. Residents and visitors were invited to bring coolers and lawn chairs to enjoy several hours of entertainment that flowed into the countdown for an incredible display of fireworks. Each year seemed to offer a bigger, better experience for those in attendance. Although, the most important aspect of July 4th for Maxie was helping to prepare the morning rededication for Veterans Memorial Park that she and others had helped raise funds to build several years before.

The memorial area located next to Aaron Bessant Park was created in a circular design with granite pedestals each about five feet tall and standing several feet apart. Each pedestal represented a military branch with the appropriate emblem for the Army, Navy, Air Force, Marines, and Coast Guard. The United States flag, Florida state flag, and POW flag flew high above on strong poles in the middle of the circle. Personalized bricks dedicated in honor or memory of military veterans covered the ground in the circle. Knockout roses and blooming shrubs decorated the perimeter of the memorial. Walkways entered memorial gates from three different directions. One from the main street that also led directly to the beach, and two from walking trails that came in one from the left and one from the right.

Each year, several days before the rededication, Maxie and a friend placed a red, white, and blue wreath on the top of each granite pedestal. Then she helped area veteran organizations put together a ceremony for residents and visitors to attend for remembering and honoring the meaning of July 4th and those who served to bring freedom to America and those who had continued forward. Her family had contributed their part, and she would do all she could to ensure that they and others would be remembered for all they had done and continue to do so that others could enjoy their July 4th picnics, fun, laughter, and freedom.

In preparation for this morning's 10:00 a.m. rededication Maxie already had donuts, bagels, coffee and table cloths packed in her car. She took the framed blue star service flag from the wall in the kitchen and placed it in the basket with framed purple hearts and photos that belonged to her father-in-law, father, husband and son. With those items she placed another framed flag that looked exactly like the blue star service flag, only it had a gold star in the center instead of a blue star. It was the symbol of a loved one like her dad that had died in a war zone. Maxie was going to create a display at the morning's event to carry on educating those who did not know the meanings of these military family symbols.

"Anything else I can do to help?" Hugh asked as he poured another cup of coffee.

"You can put this basket in the car for me if you don't mind. Is Shay dressed?"

"He should be down any second now."

About that time Shay bounded into the kitchen from his upstairs bedroom. He had already had breakfast.

"I'm ready!" he said. "I've been working on my salute to the flag all week with Grandpa."

"That's wonderful young man!" said Maxie "I'm sure you'll outshine everyone! Let's get going!"

When Maxie, Hugh, and Shay arrived at the park, volunteers had completed setting up chairs for guests and speakers, and tents and tables for snacks, beverages, and displays. The projected early morning rain had already passed over the county. People were arriving and taking seats or chatting with one another. The July heat and humidity, which kept the event short, already had volunteers handing out bottled ice water.

From a short distance Kerra saw Maxie placing something on a table. As she approached, she saw the military items.

"Good morning Maxie. What's all this?"

Kerra looked at the photos of four men in uniform behind framed military medals.

"Good morning Kerra! It's so good to see you!" Maxie stopped what she was doing and offered Kerra a hug.

"It's good to see you, too, Maxie." Kerra smiled broadly and returned Maxie's hug. "Now tell me, who are all these handsome men?"

"First, this is my father-in-law, a Soldier who was captured at the Battle of the Bulge during World War II. Fortunately he survived to return home. This is his Prisoner of War Medal. These medals didn't exist until authorized by Congress and signed into law by President Ronald Regan November 8, 1985. Our family had to request the medal, of course with proof of Pops service and capture. He died at age ninety-one at the Veterans home."

Maxie touched the next photograph. "This was my father, also a Soldier. He fought in Korea and Vietnam. He died there. I'll never forget the day the black car drove up in front of our house and two men in uniform came to the front door. I was twelve years old. When my mom and grandmother answered the knock, I heard the men say they were sorry and then hand Mom what looked like a letter. Then they just left like nothing had happened. Mom, Grandma, and I just huddled together and cried. This medal here is his Purple Heart. It is awarded to those who are injured or who die during combat. And this is his Bronze Star."

Kerra read the information that Maxie had placed inside the frame with the Bronze Star.

"Any person whom while serving in any way in or with the United States military after 6 December 1941, that distinguished himself or herself apart from his or her comrades by brave or praiseworthy achievement or service, that did not include participation in aerial flight. The act justifying award of the medal must be performed while fighting an enemy of the United States, or while involved in conflict with an opposing/foreign force. It can also be awarded for heroism while serving with friendly forces engaged in combat against an opposing military in which the United States is not a belligerent party."

"And this handsome man," said Kerra, "must be Hugh."

"Yes, that's my stern looking U.S. Marine, a young version of Dustin. Hugh was also awarded a Purple Heart for gunshot wounds and this is his Vietnam Service Medal."

"And, of course, this is Dustin during his first tour to Afghanistan."

Kerra studied the photo. Dustin was dressed in Army fatigues and flak jacket, a helmet, and holding a rifle pointed toward the ground. The background appeared to be the desert and mountains. His face was lean. He appeared tired and drained. Kerra felt a fault shutter in her heart. She had never studied the face of a combat veteran or thought too deeply about what they endured and felt in the wake of their jobs ten thousand miles from family and home. Beneath Dustin's photo lay a large frame with two Purple Hearts, a Bronze Star, and Silver Star. Kerra read the definition of the Silver Star:

"The Silver Star is the third-highest military combat decoration that can be awarded to a member of the United States Armed Forces. It is awarded for gallantry in action: While engaged in action against an enemy of the United States; While engaged in military operations involving conflict with an opposing foreign force; or while serving with friendly foreign forces engaged in an armed conflict against an opposing armed force in which the United States is not a belligerent party. Actions that merit the Silver Star must be of such a high degree that they are above those required for all other U.S. combat decorations but do not merit award of the Medal of Honor or a Service Cross (Distinguished Service Cross, the Navy Cross, or the Air Force Cross."

Kerra's thoughts returned to the comment by the girls at the dental office regarding Dustin Brites being the local hero of the current wars. She wondered what he had done that had given him such honors. Maybe sometime in the future she would ask Maxie, who was placing two framed flags on the table. One she had already seen hanging in Maxie's kitchen with the blue star. But now she had another with a gold star instead of blue.

"Maxie, what is this flag?" Kerra pointed toward the gold star.

"Oh, that's the gold star service banner. It's provided to families of those who suffer the death of a loved one who dies while on active military service to this country. This one was given to my grandmother after my dad died in Vietnam. It's a tradition that began during WWI with a group of mothers that came to be known as Gold Star Mothers of America. This lapel pin I'm wearing here on my blouse, it's called the Gold Star Lapel Button. It was designated by Congress in 1947 for immediate family members of those who died on battle fields. The laurel wreath border signifies valor, the purple field signifies the family's grief, and the gold star in the center has been used since WWI to signify a death in a combat theater. This is the flag that was folded and given to my mother at Dad's funeral." Maxie placed the flag on the table.

Kerra stood in awe of the military history and sacrifice represented by one family.

"Maxie, I'm so honored to know you and your family. I don't come from a military family, at least not in the immediate line. So this really makes July 4th more meaningful."

"My favorite quote," Maxie said as she straightened the white cloth on the table, "came from George Orwell during World War II. *'Tough men stand ready to destroy an enemy that wishes to do us harm so we can sleep safe in our beds at night.'* So many seem to have forgotten this."

"Well, thank you for reminding me," said Kerra as she watched Maxie place a framed copy of the quote on the table where others were also placing photos of their loved ones with military memorabilia.

Once finished, Maxie took Kerra by the hand.

"Come on, let's get a bottle of ice water and find Shay and Hugh. The ceremony should start shortly."

When Shay saw Kerra he jumped from the chair next to his grandfather and ran towards her. Kerra gave a welcoming smile as he wrapped his arms around her legs.

"Hello friend! I was hoping I'd see you!"

"Me, too!" squealed Shay who was wearing a red, white, and blue shirt with blue shorts and his Crocs.

Shay led Kerra by the hand to sit down between him and Maxie just as the president of the local Veterans Council approached the speaker's stand and welcomed the more than one hundred guests. A retired Navy Chaplain gave the invocation. The mayor provided a few welcoming words and then introduced the guest speaker, former Army Sergeant Dustin Brites.

Kerra felt her heart pound as Dustin stepped forward. He looked incredibly handsome in Army fatigues and cap. Then she hung onto his every word.

"I want to thank everyone for attending the 10th annual July 4th rededication ceremony of this beautiful Veterans Memorial Park. We owe great thanks to everyone who worked diligently to make this special place a reality.

For those of you in attendance today, I hope you will take time to read the names of those honored and remembered on each brick, for they signed a blank check to give their lives if necessary in defense of the Constitution of the United States, the freedom of our nation, and that of others.

Many of you in this audience today have served. Some of you have military family history back to the American Revolution and the fight for independence from England that led to the birth of our great nation. Please bear with me as I remind you of the beginning history for our nation's independence.

After a year of conflict with England, the colonies convened a Continental Congress in Philadelphia in the summer of 1776. On June 7 in the Pennsylvania State House, now Independence Hall, Richard Henry Lee of Virginia recommended a resolution with these famous words: "Resolved: That these United Colonies are, and of right ought to be, free and independent States, that they are absolved from all allegiance to the British Crown, and that all political connection between them and the State of Great Britain is, and ought to be, totally dissolved."

On June 11, a committee comprised of John Adams of Massachusetts, Roger Sherman of Connecticut, Benjamin Franklin of Pennsylvania, Robert R. Livingston of New York and Thomas Jefferson of Virginia was appointed to draft a statement for the colonies' reasoning for independence. Thomas Jefferson drafted the actual document.

The Continental Congress reconvened on July 1, 1776. On July 2, Lee's Resolution for independence was adopted by 12 of the 13 colonies. New York did not vote. Jefferson's Declaration of Independence received minor changes, and was officially adopted in the late afternoon of July 4th, 1776, with votes by nine of the thirteen colonies. Pennsylvania and South Carolina voted No. Delaware was undecided and New York abstained.

It is said that John Hancock, President of the Continental Congress, signed his name "with a great flourish" so England's King George could see it without spectacles!"

Dustin continued. "I ask that you all remember and pass it forward to all you can, especially the youth of today, that freedom did not come for free to create our nation. It came with the high cost of human life. And the same price has been paid through all the wars that our military has been asked to engage in. Let me remind everyone that although our military is the best in the world through its training and standing brotherhoods to defend our country, families, and friends, we, most of all, would prefer not to have to engage enemies. We would prefer never to see our brothers and sisters die on battlefields or live with heavy wounds in mind, body, or spirit for the rest of our lives. However, we are ready to serve when our government and necessity calls. No, freedom is not free and the name on each brick at this memorial garden is here to remind everyone of this and the meaning of this day, July 4th. And in the name of this freedom, please enjoy a wonderful picnic today and great fireworks tonight."

Dustin concluded with a thank you and disappeared behind a full and flowering magnolia tree. Everyone stood and provided a raving ovation. Kerra was spellbound by the echo of his voice, the poignant words he spoke with conviction, confidence, and clarity. Several times during Dustin's talk, their eyes had locked onto one another. Kerra wondered if Dustin's heart had fluttered like hers. She wanted to run to him, thank him, hug and kiss him for everything that she was beginning to know and understand about this man of war and community.

After the closing prayer, Dustin walked to his family and Kerra.

"Okay, Mom. Satisfied?"

"Honey! You were absolutely incredible! Maxie grabbed her son and gave him a mother's proud hug.

"No one could have done a better job, Son," Hugh said as he patted Dustin on the back.

"Well, Buddy, what do you think?"

"You did good Dad. Really good. Look who's here."

Dustin's eyes met Kerra's. "You spoke so eloquently," she said. "Thank you for your service and for reminding all of us why we celebrate July 4th."

"Thanks. Mom's been after me to be the guest speaker for a while this year. I figured I better go on and get it over with so she would stop bugging me."

"Well, I agree with your dad. No one else could have done it better. Thank you again. Could I shake the hand of a real hero?"

Kerra extended her hand to Dustin to shake hands. Although he accepted the gesture he kindly said, "I'm not a hero. Those who died on the battlefields are the real heroes. I did what I was paid to do as a Soldier, just like the others. We're just people who never know how far we can go until we're placed in situations that call for all we can do to make a positive difference."

Kerra recalled this quote from the past. The newspaper article. Dustin was the one who had saved the father and daughter that day in the gulf. He was the one who had made this statement. He was the one whose hand she had wanted to shake. Now here they stood eye to eye, hand in hand. She was so overwhelmed with emotion that she had to steady herself as that same feeling from his touch riveted through her body. Dustin, too, felt the sensation. When they released hands, Kerra turned to Maxie and Hugh. "You two have a wonderful son. And Shay, you have a wonderful dad. This was a great event."

"Are you coming for barbeque and fireworks tonight at Gammie's house?"

Kerra hesitated a moment, then Dustin spoke.

"Why don't you go hang out with everybody? I'll be on duty just in case we have any calls from fires, burns or anything else that crops up on a holiday like this."

Kerra smiled and looked back at Shay. "Okay my friend, I guess I'll see you later this evening. Maxie, is there anything I can bring?"

"Nope, just yourself, but no later than 5:30 p.m."

"Okay, I'll see you later."

Kerra walked back to the tables to look at more photos and military memorabilia. Dustin watched her with longing in his eyes and heart.

With time on her hands until going to Maxie's, Kerra returned to the cottage to make a few calls back to Wisconsin. Her family and friends had always gathered at the lake near the farm for a picnic and boating. She had always enjoyed being pulled on the air-tube behind Winston's dad's boat until after the accident. After that, the picnic and fun around the lake became an event that her immediate family had kept going for the sake of her nephews. Later in the evening they drove to Eau Claire for fireworks. When Kerra's mom answered the phone in Wisconsin, she sounded chipper.

"Hello, my middle daughter! What are you doing today?"

"Wow, you sound extraordinarily cheerful!"

"It's a beautiful warm day here at the farm and it's going to be like old times. Winston and his family are joining us for the picnic today and going for fireworks this evening in Eau Claire!"

"Oh, Mom, that's wonderful! So Winston's coming along better than doctors ever thought."

"He took a few extra steps yesterday at therapy. You've got to call him."

"I had planned on it after calling you." Kerra wiped tears of joy away from her face.

"Is Winston's dad going to bring the boat out for the kids today? I know he hasn't done that since the accident because it probably reminded him of the fun times Winston used to have."

"Actually he is. From what I understand Winston told his dad it was a must, because he wanted to watch the kids laugh and enjoy the thrills he always had. And he wants his dad to get him on the boat to do some lake fishing. So the boat's had a tune-up for our July 4th fun."

"Mom, I wish I were there with you all. I think I'm going to be missing a special day. But there's something I'd like to ask you to do for me."

"And that is…"

"First, give Winston a big hug and a kiss on the cheek for me. Second, when you say the blessing over the picnic, please have a flag and don't forget to say a prayer for all those who served and sacrificed to give us freedom, and those that still do, and also our country's first responders."

Kerra told her mom about the morning's event and all she had been reminded of that she, for the most part of her life, had taken for granted. She shared about her growing friendship with Maxie, to the extent that Maxie came from a strong military family. She wasn't ready yet to bring up to her mom anything about Dustin and how she felt when near him.

After their goodbyes, Kerra called Winston. She congratulated him on his continuing progress. They laughed and talked about old fun times and how there would be more to come.

"I'm still going to own your dad's dairy one day."

"I have no doubt," Kerra said with a smile so wide that Winston could feel it across the phone waves. "And you're also coming to visit me here at *The World's Most Beautiful Beaches*. But not in summer. It's much too hot then. I've heard fall is perfect when the monarch butterflies come through."

"Sounds like a deal," Winston laughed. "I need to get away for a while."

"Give your folks a hug for me. I hear your dad is pulling the boat out again for the kids."

"Yep. It's been too long. Got to pass the fun along like we used to have. I can't wait to watch your nephews' expressions while they're riding the air-tube and hit the wakes."

"Have someone take pictures and post them on facebook for me. Wish I were there with you all. Just know I'll be there in spirit."

"We know. What *are* you doing today?"

Kerra told Winston the same as she had told her mom, and that she would be enjoying a late evening barbeque followed by a fireworks display from the beach.

"Sounds like you'll be in good company with good food and fun," Winston said.

"Oh, I will. Make sure to give everyone at home a hug for me. I'll check on you later."

After saying goodbye, Kerra realized that Winston really was going to be okay. His old laughter had returned, and he still held to his dream of owning the farm. Kerra smiled and felt the burden that she had been carrying for so long suddenly fall from her shoulders.

After the calls, from her seat beneath her secured umbrella, Kerra watched the sand fill with various colors and sizes of umbrellas and other forms of shade from the piercing sun. The smell of sun tan lotion slathered on skin tones from the fairest to the darkest drifted on the warm air. And all size bodies from the sleek to the larger sat or lay stretched tops up and tops down on beach towels. Children and young teens laughed and giggled while they chased the surf on body boards and skim boards. Others made sand castles and creations in the sand with bright colored plastic molds, shovels, and buckets. A couple of teens buried another beneath the sand with only their head, hands and feet sticking up. Someone's stereo speakers provided alternating music genres from country to rock-in-roll. A few folks flew the United States flag where they perched in their beach chairs. There was hardly another available place for a body to sit. It was definitely a place and time to people watch. An abundance of cell phone cameras captured poses and activities. After dark everyone who had purchased fireworks would be setting them off all along the miles of gulf. Kerra had heard from Sarah and the girls at work that July 4th would be like this. This was one of the Redneck Riviera's most cherished holiday spectaculars.

At 4:00 p.m. Kerra strolled back to the cottage to shower and dress for Maxie's barbeque. This time she laid out her swimsuit to take and play in the pool with Shay. Kitten jumped on the bed where the swimsuit lay and curled up on it as though to say "I'd like for you to stay home." After her shower, Kerra pulled her wet hair back in a pony tail, put on no makeup and pulled the swimsuit on along with a pair of shorts and top. She packed a small bag with an extra set of dry cloths, shampoo, brush, and a beach towel. Maxie had said something about going down to the park after the barbeque to see the Panama City Pops Orchestra perform patriotic music and honor veterans.

When Kerra arrived at Maxie's, the older lady couldn't say thank you or smile enough when presented with a flower arrangement of red, white and blue Gerber daisies and a red, white, and blue pool float for Shay.

"Shay is going to never let go of this float," Maxie said. "And I'm going to place the flowers in a vase for the table. You go on out back. Neighbors and kids are out there at the pool. Hugh and some of the men have the grill going. He's already cooked up some spare ribs and chicken."

Kerra took the float outside and walked to the edge of the pool. It didn't take Shay long to see her.

"Miss Kerra! Did you bring your swimsuit this time?"

"I sure did! And look what else I have."

Kerra held up the float for Shay to see. "Do you think we can share this?"

"You bet!" Shay swam to the side of the pool and pulled the float into the water. Kerra walked to the small pool house where she removed her shorts and top and quickly showered before getting into the pool. Sarah was already there helping moms from the neighborhood keep an eye on the children.

"Hey girl. I'm glad you made it." Sarah said.

"I'm glad to be here. It sounded like lots of fun." Kerra entered the water. She and Sarah began throwing rings to the bottom of the pool for Shay and his friends to retrieve.

"I didn't want to miss it since this is my first July 4th at the beach."

Playing with the kids and chit chat between the women went on for another thirty minutes before Hugh called everyone out for dinner. When he saw Kerra, he rushed to her with a bear hug. Kerra returned the hug along with giving him a kiss on the side of the face.

"Hey," Kerra laughed. "I like your Hawaiian swim trunks and shirt. You're stylin'!"

"My favorite outfit for summer! Come on, you've got to try my famous spare ribs."

Everything was arranged pretty much the same on the screened porch as it had been during Shay's birthday party, except two long tables were temporarily added against one end of the room to hold all the food buffet style. And a couple of new tables with chairs covered by umbrellas had been added outside near the pool. Although there were a number of people there, Kerra hoped for some time with Maxie. She wanted to ask about Dustin. Her curiosity had risen about what he had done to be awarded a Silver Star Medal, and how he had coped after leaving the Army.

Kerra found her place in the food line in front of Maxie, who as usual, waited until everyone had a full plate before she filled her own. Kerra was headed out the door toward the vacant bistro table and two chairs when Maxie caught up with her.

"Hey, come with me to my secret place," Maxie said.

Kerra followed the petite woman to the end of the house where stairs led to the screened deck on the second floor. Two wicker rockers with side tables sat on a large tropical rug. Rubber tree plants sat in each corner. Colorful painted fish hung on either side of the glass door that allowed entrance into a bedroom. But the view straight in front of them over to the gulf and at an angle to watch the sunset was breath taking.

"Oh, my, Maxie, this takes my breath away."

"Doesn't it?"

Both women put their plates of food on the side tables and stood together for a few moments to take in the view in front of them.

"I've sat here and said many a prayer. I've laughed, and cried," said Maxie as though in thoughts far away from the moment.

Kerra didn't know what to say. Then Maxie turned her face toward Kerra's with a smile and said, "Come on, let's eat some ribs before they get cold."

The women sat down and with napkins in their laps and tucked inside the necks of their shirts, they made faces of pleasure with each bite of the scrumptious ribs that Hugh had prepared and slathered with his secret sweet sauce. Kerra finished one and wiped her lips before looking back toward Maxie.

"May I ask a personal question about Dustin?"

"What do you want to know?"

"I read the definitions of the medals that he was awarded. Those you had at the event this morning. What did Dustin do to receive such a high honor?"

"Well, according to my son, he did nothing more than his job of being there for his brothers and sisters in arms. He doesn't even believe he deserves the medals. But that's nothing unusual. Military men and women worth their salt will never brag, tell their story, or believe they do more than any other person going to work each day. Hugh always said that a quarter and one of his medals wouldn't even get him a cup of coffee, and that's pretty much true for any of our folks in uniform. But those medals stand for something more to us family members who have waited in the wings while our loved ones were out doing what the other 99.9% of the country doesn't. But maybe that's the plan God has. Everyone has a different journey and my family just happened to be on the military journey side of life. But, back to what you asked about Dustin. He was in two IED explosions that rattled his brain a good bit and sent shrapnel into his right hip and upper thigh. Then during another deployment he took a gunshot wound to his left lower abdomen. For those wounds, he received two Purple Hearts. He was awarded the Silver Star after he and part of his unit were under heavy fire and he raced to reach two of his comrades that went down. He pulled them back to cover and saved one, but couldn't keep the second one alive. As their Medic, he carried guilt for a long while. After he got out of the Army it wasn't easy here at home. Shay was only two. Dustin just wanted to lock himself away from the world. He wouldn't even go out fishing with his dad that first year. He would walk to a store and buy beer or vodka and sit here and drink. I would hear him thrashing and crying in his sleep and I knew from years ago with his dad that the only thing I could do was call his name from a far corner until he woke up. Several times when severe thunder storms came through I would find him hiding in his closet and shuddering. The greatest pain a parent carries is in knowing that they can't fix their child. That's why this is my special space. I've looked out over that horizon and watched the sun come and go while saying prayers and drying tears for my son, and all the other sons and daughters that suffer so, and the families that suffer because their children didn't return."

Kerra studied Maxie's face. Suddenly she saw lines that didn't usually come through the smile she always carried around. "Maxie, I can't imagine all that you've been through. Dustin seems to be doing so well now."

"Oh, sweetheart, he has come light years from where he was. The first year was the very worst with his sleep walking and believing enemy was still outside the windows. He still doesn't sit anywhere that his back is not against the wall. He has to see all that is surrounding him. For the first fireworks after he came home, we bought noise reduction headphones for him. When he did decide to go fishing at the pier, he only wanted to go at night. Of course the VA only wanted to fill him full of pain pills and anxiety medications. After I started reading on how they all confused one another and the brain, I went hell bent on finding different remedies. After about a year, medications were more balanced or got thrown in the toilet all together, and he returned to his first love of swimming. Now he's into yoga."

"Yoga? I love yoga!" Kerra said.

"I just knew there was something special about you," Maxie laughed. "And I know something else, too, that my son just will not admit."

"What's that?"

"I saw him watching you walk away from us this morning. His eyes were glued to you and the look on his face was like a puppy that couldn't get to its mama. I believe he knows as much as I and Shay do about how special you are, but he's afraid."

"What's he afraid of?"

"That if any of his PTSD issues rise back to the top it will frighten you away. He's had good friends whose wives and girlfriends have left them because every day isn't a perfect one for some of these guys. I know that although Dustin has come so far and he leads a much better life than many, he does get emotionally down and need space on certain dates when he's reminded of events that took friends."

"Well no day is perfect for anyone. I know that much from my own experiences."

Kerra shared with Maxie her own struggles with guilt and the story of the car accident and Winston, and her latest conversation with him today.

"You know, Kerra. I don't believe in coincidences. And I don't believe there are mistakes in the journeys of life. We're all connected, even through events with Wisconsin and Florida!"

"I believe you're right Maxie!"

The two women were laughing when they heard Hugh's voice.

"I thought I'd find you two up here. Folks downstairs are cleaning up. Are we still going to the Pops Orchestra concert ladies?"

"Yes we are," replied Maxie. "But for the next couple of minutes, let's just watch the sunset together."

Kerra rode in the car with Maxie and Shay with Hugh at the helm. Maxie had packed plenty of leftover barbeque ribs and chicken legs with side dishes to take by the Fire & Rescue Station for Dustin and the crew. After Hugh pulled into the driveway to the side of the building so not to obstruct the emergency vehicle exit, Maxie opened her car door and headed to the station entrance. When she returned, Dustin and Jason were following to retrieve the two boxes from the trunk of the car. Kerra kept her attention on Shay as they played rock, scissors, paper so she wouldn't twist her neck to get a glimpse of Dustin. Then a double tap against the car window on her left caught her attention. When she turned, Dustin was motioning for her to let the window down. As soon as Shay caught sight of his dad he couldn't hold his excitement.

"Hey Dad, Miss Kerra got in the swimming pool with me today. She even brought me a new float colored like the flag. And we've been playing paper, rock, scissors all the way over here."

"Well, sounds like you've been keeping Miss Kerra busy. You're not wearing her out are you? You don't want to scare her off."

Shay gave Kerra a serious look. "I'm not going to scare you off, am I Miss Kerra?"

Kerra smiled and stroked Shay across the head. "Absolutely not, young man. Absolutely not."

"So, did you enjoy Dad's gourmet barbeque this afternoon?"

"I did and it was the tastiest I've ever had. We have good cheese and milk in Wisconsin, but I guess you southerners have the blue ribbons for barbeque."

"Okay, Son," Maxie called from the back of the car where the trunk was raised. "Give Jason a hand with this other box and sweet tea so we can get on over to the park and hear the rest of the concert."

"Are you staying there for the fireworks?" Dustin asked as he made his way to Maxie.

"No, we'll get on back to the house and watch them from the upper deck. They're much prettier from there, and that'll get us out of the way of traffic before everyone else."

"Sounds like a good plan. I'll see you at the house in the morning."

With boxes of food and tea in hand, Dustin and Jason stopped once more to speak to Shay, Kerra and Hugh before they headed back toward the station. Hugh drove to Pier Park where he made several rounds before locating a parking spot. After gathering lawn chairs and a cooler of water from the trunk, the four made their way to the cross walk toward the outdoor amphitheater where special concerts were held throughout the year and home to the free summer concerts held on Thursday evenings. The July 4th concert with The Panama City Pops Orchestra was always outstanding. Lawn chairs and blankets covered the majority of the grassy park in front of the amphitheater. Locals that lived nearby and who had driven their golf carts to the event were parked in a special area behind the chairs and blankets. A few vendors were scattered about selling glow lights for kids, beverages and popcorn. Locals stopped and offered handshakes and hugs to others they knew from the community, which included Hugh, Maxie, and Shay being approached with smiles and short conversations, and Kerra's introduction to new faces she hadn't seen at the dental office.

Stars blanketed the night sky. And the symphony musicians glowed in the white light of the amphitheater stage. Combined with the morning's Veterans Memorial rededication, this was the most magical July 4th Kerra had experienced as she watched children play and chase one another around on the park grass, and adults talk and laugh among themselves as patriotic music wafted through the air and crossed the gulf waters just a short walk away. She felt as though she was becoming a solid part of a community. And no doubt felt like she had already fallen in love with one of the best families that chance could lead a girl to meet.

After the name of last song of the concert was announced, Kerra and Shay held hands and walked behind Maxie and Hugh to return to the car for the short drive back to the house.

"Miss Kerra, just wait till you see the fireworks from our house! It's so cool! We're above everybody on the ground!"

"I can't wait! I've never seen fireworks like that before."

In place on the upper deck at 8:55 p.m., in preparation for the 9:00 p.m. extravaganza, the fireworks still had not begun by 9:15.

"Mmmm, I wonder what's going on," Hugh said. "There usually isn't a delay unless a glitch or something happened."

Within moments the sound of a helicopter was overhead and sirens were screaming from Rescue Station One.

"Must be more than just a glitch," Maxie said, as she rocked back and forth in one of the wicker chairs. "We'll hear from Dustin in a while."

Shay sat in Kerra's lap as she rocked back and forth in the other chair. He was drifting to sleep. She looked at his face and saw his dad's features. She traced a finger across his forehead and smiled. Maxie watched her every move and smiled to herself.

"I'm going downstairs and make some decaf coffee, would anyone else like a cup?"

"No, but thanks for asking," Maxie said.

"I'm good, too," Kerra replied.

Hugh disappeared through the door that went into the bedroom attached to the upper deck.

"Kerra, I believe you would make an excellent mom."

"Well, with this one, it seems it would be pretty easy. He's so blessed to have such a wonderful family. But so sad he never knew his mom."

"We tell him about her and show him pictures. She was a wonderful young woman from a fine family. We take him to place flowers at the cross where the accident happened. Actually her birthday is tomorrow, and we'll be going to visit. We always take pictures and email them to her parents."

Kerra thought a moment as she continued rocking Shay and stroking his hair.

"Since tomorrow isn't a work day, do you think it would be okay if I came along? It sounds silly, but I'd like to let Shay's mom know what a great boy she left to share with others."

"Of course you can come. We would love that."

Suddenly the fireworks burst into the sky just as Hugh returned.

"Dustin called. He said an eight year old girl was reported missing by her family around 8:30 p.m. The entire rescue and police department had been searching for her. Thankfully she was found strolling down the beach several miles from where her family last saw her. I just can't image how something like that can happen. And I also can't imagine the panic in the parent's hearts when they realized she was missing." Hugh took a swallow of his coffee.

"I agree," said Maxie.

"Me, too," Kerra said quietly as she snuggled Shay closer to her and he continued to sleep through the most beautiful fireworks display she had ever seen.

CHAPTER FOURTEEN

On Sunday morning, after completing her yoga, Kerra sat at the cottage patio table sipping green tea and perusing through the latest *Woman's World* Magazine. She stopped and examined a page with treats for kids and wondered if Shay would enjoy making the decorated marshmallow pops on a stick. Maybe they could create these together after taking flowers to the place of the accident where his mom's life ended. Just as she was about to look for note paper to write down the items she needed to purchase, her phone rang.

"Hello, Mom! What's up?"

"Well, good morning. Just checking in to see how your July 4th went."

"I had a wonderful day and evening with my new friends and extended family. And, just so you'll know, I talked to Winston the other day and he just sounds so positive. I guess I'm finally moving forward from that dark spot I was holding on to and feeling more sun shine."

"I'm so glad, Kerra. You've held on to things you couldn't control or change no matter how deep you let yourself fall into a rabbit hole."

"I know, Mom. But you know what they say: 'Life is a journey, not a destination.' And I can only guess that the journey is for purposes of learning. Who knows?"

"So, you enjoyed your first July 4th at the beach?"

"Absolutely. Remember my new friend Maxie I told you about?"

"Yes, I do."

"I had a really good time with her family and friends. Good barbeque, an evening park concert, and great fireworks. How did everything go at the farm?"

"With the exception of your absence, it was like old times. We all, including Winston and his folks, enjoyed lots of fun and laughs. Your dad even slowed down long enough to grill the burgers and hotdogs for everyone. He brought a flag and pole out and placed it in the ground near the pier, and we all said the pledge of allegiance together before the blessing and eating. If you check your facebook page you'll see the photos your sister posted."

"Mom, that sounds awesome. Tell Dad I love him, and I hope he'll slow down enough to visit the beach in the fall when it's cool."

"I'm working on him. We'll just have to wait and see."

After Kerra and her mom completed their conversation, Kerra wrote down the ingredients she needed for the Under-the-Sea Marshmallow Pops to make with Shay.

> *20 lollipop sticks (or 10 paper straws each cut in half)*
> *20 large marshmallows*
> *1 package (12oz) light blue candy melts*
> *¼ cup graham cracker crumbs*
> *20 Cheddar Goldfish crackers*
> *40 large white pearl nonpareil sprinkles*

Afterwards, Kerra showered, dressed, and drove to the grocery store. Since she was going to meet the Brite's family at the location of the accident that had taken Shay's mother four and a half years ago, she also wanted to purchase a bouquet of flowers to place at the cross.

Inside the store, she meandered through the aisles selecting each of the items needed for the marshmallow pops. She imagined Shay's laughter as they worked together to create the goodies and share their tastes. She also imagined Shay sharing another joke that his grandfather had taught him. After placing a bag of large marshmallows in the buggy, she strolled to the floral department. Kerra examined the many varieties of colorful summer flowers wrapped in cellophane. Here she was trying to make a decision on flowers to celebrate the life of a woman she never knew except through the beautiful child she had left in the care of an incredible family. How did she, a farm girl from Wisconsin, find herself standing in another state wondering about a woman no longer laughing with the living? A woman who had conceded to provide a beautiful gift to a family whose lives had held so many uncertainties over the past number of years?

There were just too many ironies in life. The one who had faced death day to day for months on end in a foreign country thousands of miles away returned to his family. The one driving through her community at home had been struck by a car and killed. Kerra sighed and pushed away the thoughts that were becoming too deep to comprehend as she pulled a large bouquet of mixed cut flowers in colors from purple to yellow, red, orange, and fuchsia. Deep in thought as she placed the bouquet into the basket, she was startled when she heard her name called. When she turned, Dustin stood near enough to touch and Shay stood next to him.

"Hello there. You were certainly into studying those flowers," Dustin said with a slight smile. "Want to help us make a selection?"

Kerra hesitated a moment as her heart raced and Shay let go of his dad's hand to go to her.

"Today is my mom's birthday," he said. "We always get flowers for her on her birthday."

"I think that's wonderful Shay. Your Gammie told me this was a special day. Do you approve of the flowers I picked out to take?" Kerra held up the bouquet that she had placed in the basket.

"I give them two thumbs up," Shay said as he held up both thumbs.

"Well how 'bout I move away so you and your dad can pick out what you want."

After Shay and Dustin picked out bouquets of red and white roses, they walked with Kerra to the cashier, and then together to the parking lot. Anyone who didn't know would think they were a family. Before parting ways, Kerra asked Dustin a question.

"Do you and Shay have plans after the birthday remembrance?"

"We were going to the new amusement park that's being slowly returned to the beach. Shay's mother always loved cotton candy and riding the merry-go-round."

"Miss Kerra, would you come with us," Shay pleaded. "My mom's in heaven. And even if she's watching, I'm sure she won't mind."

Kerra looked at Dustin and then back at Shay.

"You can ride with us. Can't she Dad?" Shay said quickly

Dustin looked down at Shay. "Well Buddy, Miss Kerra might have other plans."

Shay looked back at Kerra waiting for her response.

Kerra didn't speak immediately. She felt that Dustin was trying to find a way around Shay's pleading without saying 'No' directly. Then she spoke.

"You know, Shay, I really appreciate the offer, but I think you and your dad should spend this special time together."

Dustin was relieved at Kerra's decision. He didn't want to cause Shay confusion by the three of them having an outing together. His mom's friendship with Kerra which flowed to Shay was one thing. But he had already made up his mind to not let his guard down and be drawn closer to her. Yes, from all he had witnessed, Kerra would be easy to love, and she would be an incredible mom. He had dreamed about kissing her passionately. But he was convinced that someone as sweet and wonderful as Kerra wouldn't be able to love him once she learned who he was as a Soldier. The things he had done in the name of war and the ghosts that often haunted his dreams.

"Okay," Shay said sadly. "But can we go together another day?"

"We'll see Buddy. Let's get going so we don't keep holding Miss Kerra up."

"I'll see you later, okay Shay?"

"Okay. But before we go, can I tell you a new joke?"

"Absolutely!"

"Okay," Shay says. "What stays in the corner but travels all over the world?"

"We don't know," both Kerra and Dustin said at the same time. "What stays in the corner but travels all over the world?"

"A stamp!" Shay exclaimed. "A stamp!"

"Oh! I get it!" Kerra laughed. "You are something else."

Dustin laughed, too. "Come on Son, we've got to go. See you later Kerra."

"You, too." Kerra watched as the two walked to Dustin's truck.

As she drove away from the store, she decided to stop at the accident location alone where she laid the bouquet of flowers. "Gloria, I never knew you. But I want you to know that you left a great gift to the world. Shay is a wonderful, beautiful little boy. Thank you for sharing." A warm breeze blew across Kerra's face and a dragon fly landed on her hand. She smiled and wondered at the possibility of Gloria being near.

After returning to her Volkswagen, Kerra called Maxie to let her know she had decided not to go with the family, but had left flowers.

"I just think it was best this time," she told Maxie. " I'll talk to you later."

At the cottage, Kerra put away the items for making the marshmallow pops. She would arrange with Maxie a time when she and Shay could visit and enjoy making the treats together. For now she was ready to curl up with Kitten on the sofa and look to see if there was anything worth watching on the movie-on-demand channel. After making a selection, she and Kitten got cozy. However, the movie didn't turn out as interesting as she thought. Kerra drifted to sleep. Two hours later she was awakened by rumbling thunder and piercing cracks of lightening.

Alarmed and dazed from waking suddenly, she walked to the window that provided her great ocean view. Thick dark clouds laden with water hung over the gulf. Surfers were taking advantage of the storm waves forming and crashing hard against the pier just down the way even though the double red warning flags flapped in wind gusts. A streak of lightening in the shape of a mountain switchback snapped from the sky to behind the horizon. Kerra changed the television station back to the weather channel to see what was happening. Tropical storm Iris was spinning around in the gulf with projected heavy rains and winds close to 60 miles per hour headed toward Panama City Beach and further inland across Florida and into Alabama and Georgia.

"Well, Kitten, it looks like we might be in for a rainy, windy night. I guess we need to bolt down the hatches."

The owners of the cottage had told Kerra that its windows were hurricane wind strength, but there were also window shutters for covering the windows for extra safety. She slipped on her flip flops. Once outside she walked against the wind to reach the two windows facing the gulf. She pressed her left hand against the shutter on the right, released its latch and then closed the shutter to cover the first window where she snapped the latches back in place on a metal frame that ran between the two windows. Then she did the same with the window on the left. As she moved around the cottage to cover the remaining four windows, palm trees flailed in the gusts and the rain began pelting against her body. She was drenched to the bone by the time the mission was complete. She could hear the waves crashing harder down at the seashore and hoped there wasn't going to be a surge that would bring the water too near the cottage, even though it was built off the ground. Attempting to see through the heavy rain, Kerra took a couple of big steps to reach the deck leading back inside the cottage. She reached to grab the railing as she lifted her right foot to meet the steps, but with wind and rain pressing against her small frame, her slippery flip flop didn't find a grip. With the loss of balance, her arms flailed and she released a scream that no one heard as she fell backwards and hit her head against a stone that was part of the walking path. For a split second she thought she could stand, but then her eyes rolled back and darkness clutched her.

Knowing that Kerra had not experienced one of their summer tropical storms, Maxie continued to call Kerra's phone number to insist she come to her home. After all the calls kept going to voice mail, she called Sarah to see if Kerra was with her.

"I've been trying to reach her as well," Sarah said.

Now they were both worried.

"I hope she wasn't out in her Volkswagen and something happened. I'm going to have Dustin go right now to see if her car is at the cottage or not. I'll get back to you."

"Did I hear my name Mom?"

"Yes you did. Sarah nor I either one can reach Kerra. She's never experienced one of these storms. I need you to go to the cottage and see if her car is there or not. If she's there, invite her to come stay here until this thing blows over. Or if she's more comfortable, take her to Sarah's apartment."

Without grabbing a rain jacket, Dustin darted out the front door and pushed against the wind toward his truck parked in front of the house. The sky grey as pewter continued dumping rain water that rushed down the street and into sidewalk drains. The tropical wind popped tree branches that landed in yards, on sidewalks and streets. Above roof lines, palm fronds swept frenziedly back and forth in the air.

Wiping rain water from his eyes and pushing his hair from his forehead with one hand, Dustin turned his truck engine with the other, turned on the headlights, and headed to the cottage. Sirens blared in the distance. He remained calm and steady, but concerned about Kerra as he dodged a thirty gallon trash can that was twirling around in the street. At the end of the street away from his family's home, he turned left onto Front Beach Road which led directly to the cottage that set on the right at the beach. With headlights on and windshield wipers slapping back and forth in high gear, traffic moved at a slow pace in the water rushing across Front Beach Road. Most tourists were experiencing the storm from patios and balconies of condominium resorts and hotels. Double beach flags were flailing in the wind to signal the severe hazard and that no one was to go into the water where waves continued to rise and crash. However, Dustin knew that inevitably someone would disregard the danger and be washed out to sea.

Ten minutes after leaving his house, Dustin pulled onto the concrete driveway at the cottage and parked next to Kerra's Volkswagen. He rushed quickly from the truck and raced around the corner of the cottage. Before he reached the steps to the deck he saw Kerra lying soaked from the rain and unconscious.

"Oh my God, Kerra!" Dustin bent to his knees and checked Kerra's airway, breathing and pulse. He placed his hand behind the back of her head that was lying against the stepping stone. He felt a gash, but there was no blood. The rain had apparently washed it away. Believing Kerra had no spinal injury Dustin scooped her into his arms and took her inside the cottage. He checked her pupils to find that her right pupil was larger than her left, a sign that she needed emergency attention for a possible concussion. He called 911 for Fire and Rescue One while he wrapped her body in the quilt that was thrown across the sofa. Then he called his mom and dad.

"I think she slipped on the steps outside the cottage and fell. It looks like she hit her head on a stepping stone. Let Sarah know. I'll call you after I know her condition. Don't get out in this weather. I'll go with Kerra in the ambulance. I just wanted you to know why she wasn't answering her phone. And Mom, do you have Kerra's parent's phone number?"

"I don't," Maxie said. She made every effort to keep her panic under control. "See if you can find Kerra's cell phone."

"Will do. The ambulance is here. Gotta go, Mom."

Dustin placed his phone back on his belt and opened the cottage door for the emergency medical technicians. Kerra lay still as a moan escaped her throat and the EMTs transferred her from the sofa to a gurney and rolled it inside the ambulance. Dustin joined her along with the technician who continued to check vitals and provide information to the hospital emergency staff.

Dustin held one of Kerra's hands and spoke close to her ear. "Kerra, come on. Wake up. Shay wants to talk to you. Mom's worried."

"Winston," Kerra whispered. "Winston."

"No Kerra, it's Dustin. You're in Florida, not Wisconsin. Do you remember?"

"My head. It's hurting. Winston, how is Winston?"

"Winston is fine," Dustin said softly. "Winston is fine in Wisconsin."

"You're in Florida, Kerra. You haven't been in a car accident. I think you slipped and fell in the rain. Do you remember?"

Kerra pressed her eyes together tight. Tears formed on her eye lashes.

"I can't remember," she said.

"You'll be okay. We've almost reached the hospital."

At the emergency room, Kerra was quickly taken into an examination room. While two nurses worked to remove the wet clothing, the doctor on duty asked questions. He and Dustin knew each other from their time on duty during emergencies.

"Does anyone know what happened?"

Dustin told him all he knew. "I don't know how long she had been laying there in the rain. I just know she has a gash on the back of head from apparently slipping and falling on wet stepping stones at her residence."

"Are you a relative?"

"No, Doc, just a friend. She's new to the area. No family here."

"Okay," the doctor said, as he checked Kerra's pupils and confirmed the pupil in the right eye was larger than the left. He looked at the nurses. "Get her wrapped warm and down stairs for a brain scan."

Dustin went to the waiting area and began pacing. He hadn't felt this anxious about a situation in a very long time. His buddies from

Fire & Rescue wished the best for Kerra before they left the emergency room. He tried flipping through a *Field and Stream* magazine, but ended up throwing it back on the table. The emergency room was filling with crying children, people in wheelchairs, and a number of those with tattoos covering their arms and legs. Dustin finally sat down. He bent his elbows to his knees and placed his thumbs between his eyes. He didn't even notice how wet his clothes were. He had gotten used to that while in Iraq and Afghanistan where he had to go for days without a dry or clean set of fatigues.

While thinking about Kerra, her smile, the way she cared for Shay and the way he felt in her presence, he heard his name called.

"Hey Dus, you okay?" It was Jason.

Dustin raised his head. Jason and Sarah stood in front of him, both with worried looks.

"Yea, I'm good. Just hope Kerra is going to be okay. She was unconscious when I found her outside the cottage. She could catch pneumonia from being in the rain, and probably has a concussion from hitting her head on a concrete stepping stone. She seems confused about where she is. She kept calling me Winston."

"Have you called her folks?" Sarah asked. "I have their number in my phone in case of an emergency."

"Let's see what the doc says before we alarm them," Dustin said. "No need in causing nerves to be shot a thousand miles away before we learn what's going on."

The wind, rain and crashes of thunder continued across the county. Several ambulances arrived with patients from auto and motorcycle accidents. Power lines were down in part of Panama City and Panama City Beach. The storm was supposed to blow through by sometime after midnight.

An hour after Kerra was taken for an MRI, the doctor returned and approached Dustin.

"Well there is good news. There is no sign of bleeding on the brain or other issues. And no spinal problems. She has experienced a concussion that seems to have left her confused. She came to enough to tell us her name. But right now she can't recall why she is in Florida. She asked if there was a car accident and wanted to know if Winston was okay. Do you know what she's talking about?"

Dustin told the doctor Kerra's story of the car accident two years before in Wisconsin and how her friend, Winston, had been left paralyzed.

"Okay, well we need to keep her several days for observation. The best thing in cases like this is total rest for a week, then a gradual pace back to normal routines so her brain can heal. You all need to go home and get some rest. She will be well taken care of."

"Doc," Dustin said, "I'd really like to stay close by. I don't want her to be here alone. She might remember me by morning."

"That's fine. I understand," replied the doctor. "It's probably best you stay in the waiting room so she's not alarmed if she wakes up and doesn't recognize you. Ease into it. The nurses can let you know when she's awake and how she responds to their questions before you enter the room."

"That's fair," Dustin said.

After the doctor walked away, Sarah suggested they go to the cafeteria and find some coffee.

"I need to call Mom and Dad, too," Dustin said as he pulled his phone from his belt to see if he had a signal from inside the hospital. "Then I need to call Kerra's folks."

Dustin pressed his mom's phone number on speed dial. When Maxie answered he shared the report given by the doctor and told her his plans for the night.

"Mom, I'm staying overnight. Can you come over in the morning? If Kerra doesn't remember me, maybe she'll remember you and Shay."

"Of course I'll be there early. You know I will. Kerra is part of our family and needs us. Are you going to call her parents?"

"Just as soon as we hang up."

"Okay, Son. Keep us posted. I love you."

"Love you, too, Mom. I'll call you after I speak to Kerra's parents."

Dustin could only hope that Kerra had mentioned his or Maxie's name to her folks so he wouldn't sound like a complete stranger when he spoke with them.

Sarah and Jason stood nearby while Dustin dialed the phone number that Sarah had provided him to call in Wisconsin.

Sylvia answered the phone. Dustin proceeded as carefully as he could to introduce himself and tell her that Kerra was hospitalized and why. He gave her the doctor's report, with an assurance that all of Kerra's new friends and extended family were close by to provide her support and care.

"I do appreciate all that everyone has done and continues to do for Kerra. I'll get a flight to Panama City Beach as soon as I can tomorrow."

"Please call and let me know your arrival time and someone from my family will pick you up from the airport."

"That's very nice of you," Sylvia replied. "I'll text you the flight information as soon as I have it."

After getting coffee and a snack from the hospital cafeteria, Dustin, Jason and Sarah sat together in the waiting room down the hall from Kerra's room. They made small talk and waited to see if a nurse would come tell them that Kerra was conscious enough to have visitors.

At 9:30 p.m. a nurse entered Kerra's room and called her name to arouse her.

"Miss Masters, I'm here to take your vitals and I have acetaminophen for your headache."

Kerra struggled to open her eyes.

"Thank you," she said weakly. "I could definitely use something for the headache and some water. And can you remind me again why I'm here?"

"A little head injury, Honey. Seems you slipped and fell backwards and hit your head on a piece of concrete. Some of your friends are outside in the waiting room. Are you up for a quick visit from them?"

"Sure. That'll be fine."

When the nurse was done, she stepped to the waiting room and let Dustin, Jason, and Sarah know that Kerra was awake for the moment if they wanted to say a quick hello.

Sarah entered the hospital room first, then Jason and Dustin. Kerra's eyes were closed.

"Hey girlfriend," Sarah said softly from the side of the bed. "You've got to stop bringing attention to yourself like this. We all love you, you know!"

"Hey, Sarah," Kerra said sleepily. Thanks for coming. Things seem kind of fuzzy right now. What in the world did I do to myself? I understand I'm not in Wisconsin anymore."

"No, you're not in Wisconsin. You're in Florida. Remember? When Dustin found you at the cottage, he said it looked like you had slipped and fell in the rain. Seems you hit your head on one of the stones of the walking path. Do you remember the fall or why you were out in the downpour?"

"I'm not sure."

Dustin stepped to the other side of the bed.

"Do you remember the ambulance ride?"

"I don't think so."

"Do you remember my name?"

"You're Dustin."

Dustin breathed a sigh of relief.

"I do believe you'll be much better in a few days. The doctor says you have to rest well for at least a week and then ease back into your normal routine. I called your mom. She will be here sometime later tomorrow."

"Hi Kerra. Remember me?"

"Your voice sounds familiar."

"It's Jason. You really had us worried. Don't be playing in the rain anymore."

"I'll try not to."

"Kerra, we're going now so you can rest," Sarah said. "We'll see you tomorrow."

"Thanks," Kerra replied quietly as she slipped back towards sleep. "Tomorrow."

After Sarah and Jason left, Dustin asked the nurse for a pillow and blanket. Since Kerra recognized him, he decided to stay in her room and nap in the recliner in the corner. Before he got himself situated in the chair, he looked at Kerra's face and wanted to touch it gently. To draw around her almond eyes and beautiful lips with his index finger. To gently push her hair back from her forehead.

Once settled with the pillow beneath his head and the thin blanket across his chest, Dustin slipped into sleep. Suddenly he heard his name called gently by a voice he hadn't heard in over five years. He sat up straight in the recliner and to his right another chair in the room had been pulled next to his.

Shay's mother, Gloria, sat beside him wearing a crisp baby blue cotton dress that she always loved. Her blonde hair was pulled up in a clip and she held a bouquet of white and red roses just like the ones he and Shay had left at the accident site for her birthday.

"Gloria, why are you here?" Dustin asked as he remained composed. He had experienced the return of comrades and friends who had died on the battlefield to let him know they were okay. He and other comrades had shared their stories with one another, but that was as far as it went for fear they would be deemed off their rockers for sure.

"Oh, sweet Dustin," Gloria smiled in reply. "I'm here for you and Shay. And Kerra. By the way, thanks so much for always remembering me on special days and for telling Shay about me. I always love the flowers you both leave by the cross where the accident happened. And it was so sweet of Kerra to leave a bouquet this morning before the storm and tell me how special Shay is. You know, I suppose if I had to leave the physical world, a place of remembrance in sight of the most beautiful beaches in the world is perfect. I sit there all the time."

"How can you be smiling so? It should have been me that died," Dustin said as he looked into her eyes. The same ones that Shay carried on for her. "I was in the most dangerous places in the world, yet I lived."

"Oh my dearest friend Dustin." Gloria placed her hand against the side of his face. "Don't question destiny or the master plan. You'll just become more confused. Just accept that we each have a journey and purpose for the here and now, and when that is finished we cross beyond a veil where we learn more than we could have ever known or understood while on earth."

"But you still haven't told me exactly why you're here," said Dustin.

Gloria smiled as the white aura grew stronger around her. "See that beautiful woman lying there resting? She's your destiny, Dustin. She's Shay's destiny. I haven't learned yet why I was taken from Shay's earthly life, but I do know that Kerra is the mom he deserves now and the woman that will make you a happy man. Remember Dustin, when you asked me to carry your child in the event of your death in combat? I cared for you so much that I was willing to do that for all the right reasons. So that a part of you would be left behind for your family. None of us knew how life was going to turn out. But we made a plan just in case. And yes, it is true. If you want to make God laugh, just make a plan. Ironically, a piece of me is now left behind and I want him to have all the happiness and joy he can experience on his journey. And Kerra has been brought into your and Shay's life for that purpose. Stop doubting yourself and fearing you can't be loved again. Or that you can't open your heart to offer more love. You are worthy of love Dustin. Both receiving and giving. Now it's your turn to care enough for me to believe what I'm saying."

Nothing you did in combat was anything you wanted to do. You did it because you were called by those above you to do it. You believed in the fight against evil and protection of the innocent and your country and family. Never forget the children and families in those countries that came to depend on you and your buddies for their safety. For giving them water, candy, toys, instruments, music, and school supplies they needed. You served Dustin, and you served gallantly and prayerfully. I'm here Dustin to say let the dust of the desert fall from your soul and let love and peace go into the places of your heart that you're trying so hard to protect from further pain or disappointment. I promise that Kerra is the one that can reopen those places for you, and bring much joy for you and Shay. And Shay most of all can continue to provide you with love and joy like nothing else. Family, Dustin, never forget that no matter where a man's journey takes him, family and love are the ultimate force on earth, but it requires work and letting go of things that hammer down peace, joy and happiness."

"But I don't deserve to love or be loved. Or to be joyful. My buddies who didn't come home, they don't get the chance to continue on with their families, fall in love, hold their kids, and laugh again."

"You might reconsider those thoughts." said Gloria. "If you had died, would you have wanted your best friends who fought to your left and right to remain in a "rabbit hole" and not carry on with life to its fullest? To not fulfill their journey?"

"No. Of course not," Dustin said demurely as he looked down at the floor.

"Well, they don't either. But they do appreciate the bracelets you keep in the box with the velvet cloth. They appreciate being remembered. But they are at peace in their new world, just like I am. I know that for those still living on earth there is no comprehension of what is beyond here. Just remember that to love and be loved, to show love in even the smallest ways for all the time that one exists on earth, and to serve one another with love is the purpose. The greatest gift you can give to honor your comrades is to carry on with the same strength and courage and to give as much of yourself to help others as you did alongside them on the battlefield."

"Dustin, forgive yourself, God already has. And He will help you through the rest of your journey, I promise. Even on the days that hurt the most when you think of one of your buddies that died or was critically injured on a given day. It wasn't God's fault. It wasn't your fault. Life on earth is what it is. A journey of spiritual beings experiencing the physical. It's only through the darkest moments that God can shine the brightest and bring peace and comfort to earthbound hearts. How else would anyone one on earth really know Him? "

"You know, Dustin, faith is easy when life seems perfect. But true faith is when the darkest experiences try to bury us, but we let God's love and light shine through anyway. It actually kind of dumbfounds some people. I find it fascinating!"

Gloria kissed Dustin on the side of his face.

"Thanks Dus for being such a great dad. I've watched you and your parents with Shay. I couldn't be prouder. He's my gift to the world. He was my purpose. I've left him to those of you I trust most."

Dustin watched as Gloria walked to Kerra's bedside, touch her on the forehead, leave a red rose on the blanket covering Kerra's stomach, and then slowly exit the room.

CHAPTER FIFTEEN

Maxie arrived at the hospital at 7:30 a.m. She hadn't seen Dustin sleep so sound since his return home from Army life. She wasn't sure whether to wake him or let him continue to sleep. Kerra was also sleeping. They both looked peaceful for all they had been through the day before.

The storm had blown over during the night and nothing but blue sky was expected for the day. Of course debris had to be cleaned up from the streets and neighborhoods. Outside Panama City Beach in the rural zones, dirt roads were washed out and causing problems for residents of that area. Power was being restored and thankfully, as of yet, there was no report of anyone being lost to sea because they disregarded the danger of the gulf waters yesterday.

Just as a nurse entered to check Kerra's vitals, Dustin sat up, stretched out his arms, and yawned.

"Well good morning, Son. You looked peaceful in that corner there."

"Mornin' Mom. A recliner chair is pretty comfortable after sleeping on the top of a Humvee for nights on end."

"Here, I brought you some coffee from home."

Maxie handed Dustin his favorite travel cup with black coffee.

"Let's go to the hall while the nurse takes Kerra's vitals," Maxie said.

"No, don't do that. You better come over here Mrs. Maxie Brites."

Maxie and Dustin turned to Kerra. She wore a smile as broad as her thin face.

"Oh, Honey, you had us so worried. I've been praying all night that God would send an angel to touch you and get you out of this place as soon as possible."

Dustin stood next to his mom. He reached and picked up the single red rose.

"Mom, did you bring this in with you?"

"I didn't. I thought maybe you placed it there."

The nurse that had entered the room exhibited a broad smile. "Well, now, how are you doing this morning, Miss Kerra? Your coloring looks much better!"

"Have you seen anyone this morning that would have left this rose on the bed?" asked Dustin.

"Oh, that would be me. A family left a large vase of red roses at the nurse's desk and as the night nurse I like to share them with the patients. Just a reminder that it's a beautiful new day for love to blossom just a little more."

Dustin looked at the nurse's name badge. It read: Gloria.

"I'm getting ready to go home now," she said cheerfully.

"Kerra I know you'll heal up in a hurry and get back to all the things you love. Another nurse will check in with you shortly. You all take care. And don't let me catch you up here again, maybe unless it's on the new mom and baby floor." Then she disappeared from the room.

Maxie looked at Dustin and then Kerra.

"Well, she was a bit *something else!*"

"Yes, she was," said Dustin. He smiled to himself as he remembered his dream. And then he looked down at Kerra.

"Hey, what's your name, age, and date of birth?"

Kerra answered the questions without hesitation.

"What state are you in now and what state did you come from?"

Again Kerra responded with no problem.

"Who is Winston and what happened to him?"

"He's my best friend in Wisconsin. We were in a car accident together. Winston was paralyzed but is making great progress now."

"And what happened yesterday?"

"I was out in the heavy winds when the rain started. I was closing the window shutters. When I started back up the steps to the deck my foot slipped from my flip flop and I fell backwards. I hit my head on the concrete stone."

"You're back!" Dustin grinned ear to ear.

"But how did I get here. Who found me?"

"When I couldn't reach you by phone," Maxie said, "I sent Dustin to the cottage to check on you. That's when he discovered you laying in the rain unconscious. He called Fire and Rescue and rode in the ambulance with you to the hospital. He's been with you since 4:00 p.m. yesterday."

"See, there you did it again," said Kerra. "You were the hero. Thank you for being *my hero* this time."

"Nope, no hero here. Just doing my job." Dustin tried to remain detached and humble. But he already knew that detaching himself from Kerra was not going to happen. He knew he didn't want to lose her.

Kerra was napping later that afternoon when her parents arrived from Wisconsin. When they entered the hospital room, they saw Maxie and Dustin sitting like guardians. To not waken her, the four walked back to the waiting room and made introductions. While talking, a nurse came. "Miss Masters is awake now if you'd like to see her."

"So, this is what it took to get both of you to visit the beach?" Kerra joked with her parents.

"Hey, we were making plans to get here in the fall, but you seem to have a way of getting our attention," her dad said with gentle sarcasm and relief that his daughter was going to be fine.

"You've got to stop taking hits to the head though, or we're going to order a special helmet for you to wear at all times!"

Everyone laughed, even the nurse that had come in to see if Kerra needed anything.

"Well," Maxie said, "Dustin and I should go so you can spend time with your daughter."

"No, don't leave," Kerra pleaded.

"Hey, we'll be back later, after dinner, and bring Shay and Dad. Deal?" said Dustin.

"Deal."

"But, before we go," said Dustin, "If Kerra doesn't mind, I would like to ask Mr. Masters something."

Dustin turned his eyes to Kerra and she returned a quizzical look with a shrug of her shoulders. Then in his most respectful military manner he said, "Sir, if your daughter will accept, would you and your wife allow me to take her on a date after she fully recovers?"

Maxie placed her hand against her mouth to keep from expelling a happy squeal. Sylvia smiled and squeezed Kerra's hand that she had been holding since she arrived. From sheer surprise, Kerra bit her bottom lip and almost forgot to breathe.

Kerra's dad extended a handshake to Dustin.

"Dustin, Sylvia and I would be happy to have you ask our daughter out. At least we know she would be safe with a medic around. But I think the final answer has to come from Kerra."

Everyone looked at Kerra. She finally exhaled and with a very serious look across her face said slowly, "Well, I might have to think on it awhile." Then she paused.

Dustin's heart began to sink as he looked toward Maxie and sucked in a breath. He was about to speak when Kerra squealed, "Absolutely!"

"Dustin," she said, "Would you come here for just a second?"

Slightly blushing, Dustin stepped to the side of Kerra's bed. She lifted her arms to him.

Dustin bent over her with a hand on either side of her pillow. Without caring if she pulled the intravenous needle from her left arm, Kerra put both arms around his neck and pulled his face to hers.

"Thank you, for everything," she said. Then she brought his lips to hers.

After observation for seventy-two hours, Kerra left the hospital. She now had a personal doctor for follow-ups if headaches, dizziness, or other issues arose unexpectedly. She had orders to rest for the first week. If all was well at the beginning of the second week, she could return to work part time.

Back at the cottage, Kerra received complete pampering by her parents, Maxie and Dustin. Winston called with inspirational words and updates on Big Red. She never felt happier. Sylvia Masters and Maxie Brites enjoyed time together getting to know one another while Hugh took Kerra's dad deep sea fishing.

During Kerra's second week back at work part time, she and Shay made the Under-the-Sea Marshmallow Pops.

"Miss Kerra, this is the coolest project ever!" Shay exclaimed as he put the straws into the marshmallows and dipped them into the melted blue candy chips.

"I'm so glad you're having fun," Kerra said, and showed him how to press the marshmallows into crushed graham crackers that represented sand, followed by placing a Goldfish cracker on the side.

"Want to take a plate of these out to Grammie and Sylvia?"

"Sure!" Shay held a plate with a few of the treats to take outside for Maxie and Sylvia. They were lounging beneath an umbrella sipping a new drink called Summer Wind.

"Ladies, how are your drinks?" Kerra asked.

"Wonderful! They both chimed.

"I suppose you got the recipe from *Woman's Day* magazine," Sylvia said.

"How did you guess, Mom?"

"Well, every time you come up with something new, it's from *Woman's World.*"

"What's in this?" Maxie asked.

"Oh, it's very healthy." Kerra laughed. "It has blended blueberries, strawberries, fresh orange juice, pineapple juice, Jamaican rum, and coconut cream."

"Well, I hope you have more," said Maxie.

"No problem!"

"Miss Sylvia, look what I have for you and Gammie. Me and Miss Kerra made them."

"Oh these look great Shay!" Sylvia exclaimed. "And I love marshmallows."

"Good job Shay," Maxie told her grandson. "Can I have one?"

"Sure Gammie." Shay turned from Sylvia to Maxie.

After he put the empty plate down, he said, "Miss Sylvia, can I tell you a joke?"

"Well of course you can. I'd love to hear a joke that I can take back to my grandsons in Wisconsin."

"Okay, here goes. What do you call bears with no ears?"

"We don't know," chimed the three women, "What do you call bears with no ears?"

"B," you sillies! Shay broke into laughter.

Sylvia and Maxie looked at one another and shrugged their shoulders. "We don't get it."

"Okay," said Shay. "Bears is spelled b-e-a-r-s. If you take off the e-a-r-s you only have B!"

"You are one smart cookie, Mr. Shay," Sylvia said. "I can't wait to tell that joke to my grandsons."

"I hope they like it," said Shay. "If they ever visit, I have lots more." Then he ran back inside the cottage to find Kitten.

Sylvia directed her attention to Kerra. "Well, my middle daughter, I can certainly see why you fell in love with Panama City Beach and your new family. What a beautiful place to live with such an incredible view. Actually, more than one incredible view."

Sylvia stared towards the water at a figure walking toward them with a kayak. Maxie smiled as her son came closer. Kerra turned and smiled to see Dustin. He placed his kayak on the sand, then bent over and kissed Kerra on top of her head.

"How you feeling?"

"I couldn't be better," Kerra lifted her chin toward him and smiled.

Dustin had not missed a day checking in on Kerra since the fall. Sarah and Jason were also daily visitors and seemed to have something going on that Kerra hadn't delved into yet. She and Dustin had been finding quiet times to talk and realize that they had each been placed on a journey they could have never dreamed up for themselves. But they felt right with one another and believed they could have a future together even if shadows of the past fell into their laps now and then. They had the love and support of family, unlike so many who didn't.

"So, Sylvia, you leave to return to Wisconsin tomorrow morning?" asked Maxie.

"I do. To my regret. But hopefully will return before too long with my husband and other friends and family." Sylvia winked at Maxie, who smiled slyly.

"Well tonight its dinner for everyone at the Brite's home," said Maxie. "Not for a goodbye, but a see you later!"

"Sounds wonderful," Sylvia said as she and Maxie toasted one another with their Summer Wind.

CHAPTER SIXTEEN

During Kerra's recuperation, Dustin had been spinning around various ideas about the perfect date with Kerra. He turned to Jason for help.

"Hey, Dude, can you give me some ideas for a great first date with Kerra."

"Well," Jason said while putting wax on the rescue truck, "for a woman like Kerra, think outside the box. She loves the outdoors, so you could do a sunset beach picnic with flambeaus, champagne, cheese and crackers. Or, you could take her out on my sailboat for a sunset sail and champagne."

"I knew you'd have the best answer. I like the sailboat idea," Dustin said. "Thanks, you're the man!"

After Kerra was cleared by her doctor for full time work, she called Dustin.

"So, I owe you a date as I recall," he said.

"That's also what I recall. You're not going to change your mind, are you?

"Not a chance. I'll see you on Sunday evening about 5:00 p.m."

"And where are we going?"

"Well, that's a surprise."

"Oh, no! Don't keep me in suspense!"

"I think you'll like my plan. Just give me a chance."

"Okay. I can't wait."

"Same here," said Dustin.

On Sunday, Maxie helped Dustin pack a picnic basket with champagne and glasses, strawberries with chocolate dip, cheese, wheat crackers and green seedless grapes. They added candles and a table cloth, dinner napkins and plates.

Before leaving the house, he hugged his mom. "Okay, I'm nervous, but I'm going to give this a try.

"You'll be fine, Son. You and Kerra are meant for one another. I feel it in my bones. Now, go. Have a good time. I can't wait to hear how much of a surprise the sunset sail turns out to be for Kerra."

After entering his truck, Dustin called Kerra. "Hey, I'm on the way. Dress comfortably and bring a sweater. This isn't a restaurant date."

After reaching the cottage, Dustin went to the door and knocked.

"I'm ready." Excitement danced in Kerra's voice. She was dressed in white shorts, a red tank top, and a black sweater across her shoulders. Dustin scanned her from the top of her head to her pink toenails. "You look awesome," he said.

"As you do, Sir. Nothing like a good looking tanned guy in Oakley swim-trunks and a muscle shirt."

Dustin, a foot taller than Kerra, dropped his face to hers and planted a quick kiss on her lips. In the truck, Kerra slid close to him.

"Okay, I hope you like surprises."

"I do like surprises and anything that's fun. And I can honestly say it's been a long time since I've really had fun. I mean real fun. I've been looking so forward to this."

"I know what you mean. So, we're starting a new day for both of us."

Within minutes Dustin pulled up to a small house where the backyard met with water and a boat dock.

"Who lives here?" Kerra asked.

"This is Jason's place."

"Really. Nice."

"Just follow me." Dustin removed the picnic basket from the back of the truck.

Kerra couldn't imagine what Dustin was up to. A picnic at Jason's? Then she saw the sailboat at the dock. The multi-colored sail was up and ready to go.

"Wait here a sec while I step in and put this basket down."

After Dustin placed the basket in a safe place, he reached a hand to Kerra and helped her step into the sloop.

"How does a sunset sail date sound?"

"Dustin Brites, I think it is the most romantic first official date anyone could have!"

"Okay, sit right here opposite me and don't make me strap you on to keep you from falling again, got it?" Dustin laughed.

"Yes sir, captain!" Kerra gave a salute. "I guess we should have brought a helmet for precaution!"

Dustin took a seat forward of the tiller to steer the 17 foot sloop. Jason spent two years building the craft that had room for two to sleep..

Since there was little wind, Dustin used the sailboat's motor to move into the bay and on to the gulf. Kerra loved the feel of the wind on her face as the boat moved forward. She closed her eyes and smiled to herself. With the tiller connected to the rudder, she felt the water as it flowed below the boat.

"What are you thinking about?" Dustin asked.

"Oh, just what a lucky girl I am for destiny to have brought me here and to this moment."

"I'm glad for that, too," said Dustin as he guided the boat out of the bay and to the west.

"I'll find a place to anchor where I hope we can see dolphins and sea turtles along with the sunset," Dustin said.

The sun still hung in the sky an hour away from falling behind the horizon.

"Okay, I'm throwing anchor here," Dustin said. They were past the county pier where some dolphins were already arcing.

Once the anchor was secured and the boat stable, Dustin took Kerra's hand and led her to sit on the bow. He pulled the table cloth from the picnic basket and placed it on the bow next to Kerra, then added the matching napkins and two champagne glasses.

"I hope you like champagne and chocolate covered strawberries," he said as he removed the bottle of Sparkling Champagne and popped the cork.

Kerra could hardly find her voice. "This is just wonderful, Dustin. Everything is perfect."

"I had hoped you wouldn't be disappointed. I wanted to do something as unique and wonderful as you." Dustin gently moved a piece of hair from Kerra's face to behind her ear. Then he placed his hand softly against the back of her head and gently pulled her face close to his where their lips met. Neither had ever felt this depth of passion.

After their lips parted from one another, they both sighed deeply.

"I hope you didn't mind my doing that."

"Anytime you like," smiled Kerra. "Except for this moment. ˙I believe I'm ready for champagne and whatever else you brought along in that basket."

Dustin pulled out the two candles and lit them. Then he sat down on the bow close to Kerra to share their picnic while the sun melted into a soothing abstract of pastels spreading across the sky.

CHAPTER SEVENTEEN

As September arrived, the daily average ninety-degree temperature plus the added heat index began dipping into the eighties. With schools back in session across the country, beach traffic had also dipped, although out of state car tags could still be spotted in beach and store parking lots. Canadian license plates and those from northern states appeared as snowbirds arrived to escape freezing winters and the abundance of snow.

Kerra enjoyed being back at work full time. Except for the occasional headache controlled by medication, she had not been affected by any other issues. She still enjoyed her walk from the cottage to work in the mornings, and the return walk home. Only now, when Dustin was on duty, she could stop Fire and Rescue to give him a morning and afternoon kiss. Of course Dustin was ribbed by crew members, but he and Kerra didn't care.

Although she and Dustin had been a tight item only since the accident, everyone believed deeply that they were meant for one another. "Just go ahead and plan a wedding," everyone said. But Dustin would shake his head with a grin and say, "Just give us time. Can't rush into these things. Kerra's got to get to know the *other* me!" And what he meant by that was the side of him that could come out of nowhere because of triggers like dreams, memories, smells, or sounds. Dustin had talked to Kerra about these things, but she had not seen any sign of a man she couldn't and wouldn't always love, no matter what.

"You can't scare me away," Kerra always said when he shared things a combat veteran brought home from war. "I will always love *both* of you."

"That's what you think, now. Wait 'til you have to wake me up from sleep walking to keep me from going out the door to look for the enemy."

But Kerra remained confident as she and Dustin moved forward. And she gained tips from Maxie regarding the space often needed by Dustin and veterans like him. Maxie had already given her notice that there were a couple of days in September and February that sometimes took Dustin off the grid. These were days that reminded him of events on the battlefield when friends were killed in action. Kerra had marked the date in September on her calendar. And today was that day. She and Dustin had made plans to go someplace together to take his mind off the memories. They agreed it would be their first sort of test to see how as a couple he would handle anxiety if it crept up like it had in the past.

Dustin tossed and turned all night. He was soaked head to toe with sweat, and so were his bed sheets. He looked at the clock on the bedside table. It was 4:00 a.m. The same time that the suicide bomber had made it through a checkpoint during one of his tours in Iraq and turned two of his friends into flying parts. Dustin went to his bathroom and turned on the shower. He let the water remain cold and fall down his body to help cool him and maybe help him settle his internal shaking. For the sake of his job that he dearly loved, he had let go of anxiety medications a while back. So he had no recourse but to do what he always did. Escape with his kayak to his quiet zone down at Ecofina Creek. No noise, no sirens, no voices, or helicopters, especially helicopters whether commercial or military, that often flew over Panama City Beach. Helicopters were only another reminder of medivacs taking friends from the combat zone or the need of them to fire against enemy to help the boots on the ground.

Kayaking down Ecofina was his ritual on a day when such memories flooded his mind. And because of this, he had totally forgotten that he and Kerra had agreed to spend the day together for their *test*.

By 4:30 a.m., Dustin had his kayak and a cooler in the back of his truck. To try and escape snapshots from his mind, he turned up a CD by AC/DC as loud as he could stand it. He stopped at a gas station and purchased crackers, water, Red Bull, and a few beers.

On his wrist he wore engraved bracelets to honor the two friends who had died in front of him on this date several years before. When he arrived at the parking lot for Ecofina Park, he removed the silver fleur-de-leis hanging on a chain and his dog tags from the truck's rearview mirror and placed them around his neck. He walked to the back of his truck, pulled out the kayak and cooler of beverages and headed down sandy path toward the water. As dawn broke, the sounds of birds chirping entered the morning along with scampering squirrels and other critters hiding in the trees and underbrush. Dustin placed the kayak in the river with the cooler attached on the back. Once he was settled inside the seat, he paddled away from the dock and into his personal place to honor his brothers with Red Bull and beer, and a *Toujours-Pret, Always Ready.*

Kerra woke early for her yoga, tea and bagel before getting ready for the planned day with Dustin. The day included driving to Cape San Blas for horse-back riding on the beach and then on to St. George's Island for a late lunch. Although Dustin was more than familiar with both locations within one hundred miles east of Panama City Beach, this would be Kerra's first time to visit. And even though she was looking forward to their day together, Kerra held no preconceived ideas of how the day would go since the date held deep wounds that would never totally heal for Dustin.

After dressing, while waiting on Dustin to arrive, Kerra sat outside to enjoy the now cooler mornings and almost empty beach in front of the cottage. After flipping through all the pages of a new magazine, she looked at her watch. Because Cape San Blas was on Eastern Standard Time and Panama City Beach was Central Time, Dustin had wanted to leave at 8:30 a.m. Central. It was already 9:00 a.m. and she had not heard from him. She called his cell number, but there was no answer. After a text, there was still no response. After a couple more attempts to reach Dustin, Kerra called Maxie.

Maxie recognized Kerra's phone number on her phone's caller I.D.

"Good morning, Sweetness, how are you this morning?"

"Hi, Maxie. I'm fine. How are you?"

"I'm my old spindly self. But the tone in your voice doesn't sound fine. Is something wrong?"

"Maxie, Dustin hasn't gotten here to pick me up for our day out together, you know, for our *test* since this is one of those bad days for him. He's not answering his phone or returning my messages. Have you seen him this morning?"

"Kerra, knowing Dustin as I do, he probably forgot about your plan. I mean *really forgot.* Not on purpose. But because these particular days have become such a part of him, that he's created his own rituals to honor his fallen brothers. I can tell you that he had placed his sheets in the laundry room this morning. They were soaked from his sweat. So that tells me he had a bad night and left the house early this morning. Please don't be upset at him."

"Oh, Maxie, that would never cross my mind. I just hope he's okay."

"Honey, I assure you, he'll show back up later this evening. He has never told us where he goes or what he does, but he will be back."

"Thanks, Maxie. I'll be waiting for him with open arms."

CHAPTER EIGHTEEN

Dustin paddled his kayak for two hours and parked at the place where he always went on this date. The beautiful white sand bar had deer tracks and signs of other animal life that lived there. The sun fell in between the canopy of oaks, magnolias, and sand pines and left sparkles dancing on the water. He placed a photo of each of his friends in the sand, and with his finger he wrote their names: Specialist Timothy Meres and Private First Class Sam North. He opened three beers and three cans of Red Bull. He placed one each beside the photos, and then had one of each for himself. He lifted his beer into the air. *"Toujours Pret,* Always Ready Brothers! Never Forgotten! I'll see you at Fiddler's Green!"

When remembering their fallen brothers and sisters, Cavalry Soldiers always referred to a poem called Fiddler's Green by an unknown author. Dustin had a copy of it with him.

The Cavalryman's Poem

Halfway down the trail to Hell,
In a shady meadow green
Are the Souls of all dead troopers camped,
Near a good old-time canteen.
And this eternal resting place
Is known as Fiddlers' Green.
Marching past, straight through to Hell
The Infantry are seen

Accompanied by the Engineers,
Artillery and Marines,
For none but the shades of Cavalrymen
Dismount at Fiddlers' Green.

Though some go curving down the trail
To seek a warmer scene.
No trooper ever gets to Hell
Ere he's emptied his canteen.
And so rides back to drink again
With friends at Fiddlers' Green.

And so when man and horse go down
Beneath a saber keen,
Or in a roaring charge of fierce melee
You stop a bullet clean,
And the hostiles come to get your scalp,
Just empty your canteen,
And put your pistol to your head
And go to Fiddlers' Green.

Dismount at Fiddlers' Green.

Though some go curving down the trail
To seek a warmer scene.
No trooper ever gets to Hell
Ere he's emptied his canteen.
And so rides back to drink again
With friends at Fiddlers' Green.

And so when man and horse go down
Beneath a saber keen,
Or in a roaring charge of fierce melee
You stop a bullet clean,
And the hostiles come to get your scalp,
Just empty your canteen,
And put your pistol to your head
And go to Fiddlers' Green.

Before dark, Dustin arrived at home where Maxie greeted him with a smile and hug. "Hi, Son. Glad you're back."

"Mom, I wonder if it's ever going to get any easier."

"Sure it will, Son. Time, it's all about the passing of time and acceptance. Which doesn't mean we like the bad things that happen to us, but we have to gain acceptance so we can move forward. What happens doesn't define who we are. What happens is just part of the thousands of threads that make up the tapestry of who we are."

"Mom, I love you. You are so wise. Sorry about the sheets, again. I'm glad you put that water proof mattress cover on the bed."

"Oh, don't worry about stuff like that. That's the least of things."

"I'm going up for a shower. I'll see you in a few."

When Dustin entered his bedroom, he saw his cell phone on the dresser. The message light was blinking. He listened to Kerra's message. "Damn," he said, and clinched his fists. He couldn't believe he had totally forgotten their plan for the day. Their *test.*

"This just isn't going to work," he told himself. "She's going to hate me."

Dustin showered quickly, dressed, and almost ran down stairs to the kitchen where Maxie was cooking dinner.

"Mom, I can't believe I totally zoned out today. Kerra and I had plans and I let her down. I told you, it could take me years to break these patterns. She's not going to want this in her life."

"Dustin," Maxie snapped. "Calm down right this minute. Give yourself a chance. Stop having preconceived ideas. Call her right now and tell her you're on the way."

When Dustin arrived at the cottage, he didn't let Kerra speak before he began apologizing.

"Kerra, I am so, so sorry. I knew this was going to happen. I didn't even give a thought to you this morning. I knew the day would come when I'd screw up. I can't be doing this to you. I knew I should have never allowed myself to fall in love. After a while, you'll get tired of my highs and lows, my forgetting things and…"

Kerra put her index finger to Dustin's lips.

"Dustin, what are you talking about? Is this more about you not trusting yourself or that you don't trust me to love you, both sides of you?"

"Kerra, I've learned too much from other combat vets that I've been in group therapy with. Their wives, fiances, and girlfriends end up leaving."

"But Dustin, we are not everyone else. We have so much going for us. Family. Yours, mine. Please don't close me out now. We've been doing so well."

"Kerra, I love you, but I'm not the right guy for you. I'll end up making you hate me. You do know I still have to see a therapist at times."

"So what," Kerra said. "Even I had to do that for a while after my car accident."

"But this is different. I may be doing it for the rest of my life."

"And that's okay, Dustin. I love you!"

"I've got to go."

"Dustin, please don't leave this way. You can't let one incident between us define what our entire future could be."

"Kerra, I'm sorry. I have to go, now."

With Dustin out of sight, Kerra sat on the sofa with her arms wrapped around her knees and pulled against her forehead. She had never cried so hard.

At work the next day, Sarah recognized that Kerra wasn't herself. Word soon spread that Dustin had pushed away from her. Maxie called and ask Kerra to give Dustin some time. But a month later, nothing had changed.

"I'm returning to Wisconsin," Kerra told Maxie and Sarah one Saturday when they were together for lunch. "This just hurts too, much." And Kerra's tears flowed again. "If I thought there was a chance that Dustin would come around, I'd stay. But I believe he is truly where he wants to be in life out of his own fears."

"I wish I could do something to help," said Maxie. "But he's not even talking much to me or his dad these days. He works, he takes Shay out for activities, he doodles with the house and that old truck, and he exercises like a mad man. And when Shay asks about you, he finds some excuse to get off the hook."

"I hope he'll let me see Shay before I leave," Kerra said as she stirred the straw around in her glass of water.

"I'll see what I can do," Maxie said.

When Maxie returned home, Dustin was on a ladder painting the house fascia.

"Dustin Brites," she called out. "There's something you might or might not care to know. Kerra is packing to return to Wisconsin. Son of mine, I love and adore you, but you're a darn fool if you let that woman go. Her kind of woman doesn't come around very often. You're keeping Shay from having someone that will adore and love him as much as any birthing mother. And one day down the road when your dad and I are gone, and Shay is grown, you're gonna wish you hadn't been so stubborn and let this one get away. Now, I've said all I'm going to say, except for I'll leave it to you to get some sense in your head or have regret and kick yourself in the butt somewhere down the road."

Dustin had stopped painting to be courteous enough to look down and listen to his mother. When she disappeared inside the house, he put the paint brush on the pan, and shook his head. He stepped further up the ladder and moved onto the highest point of the roof of the house where he sat down and peered out over the gulf.

"Damn it, damn it, damn it," he said to himself.

While contemplating all his mom had said, his cell phone rang.

"Hey, Brites, it's Sergeant Brule. What's going on, man?"

"Been a while, Brule. Sorry I haven't called you lately. How are things going?"

"Got some news for you. I'm getting' married man! I wanted to know if you'd be my best man."

"Are you kidding! You're gonna do it. After all you've been through? You were already given one set of divorce papers."

"Yep, hey, we only go around once, right, with or without legs! The first wife knew me only with *real* legs. This one has never known me with all my *real* body parts. Patty knows me only as her bionic prosthetic man! She's awesome. And great with my son!"

Suddenly Dustin felt like he'd been hit with a ton of bricks. He hadn't lost his legs, but Brule had. Here was a buddy who had fought hard to rise to the top of the pile from all the medical and mental issues he had been through. And then the additional mind bending issue when his first wife divorced him and signed all rights of a son over to him.

"I'd be honored to be your best man. Just tell me when."

"December, man. We want a Christmas wedding."

"Sounds good, Brule. I'll be there. Just send the info."

Dustin sat contemplating for a few moments before he scampered down the ladder as fast as possible and jumped into his truck. When he pulled next to Kerra's Volkswagen, he took a deep breath, closed his eyes, and said a prayer. When he knocked at the cottage door, it didn't take but a moment for Kerra to appear. Pure surprise and shock covered her face.

"Can I come in?"

Kerra opened the door, but didn't say anything.

"I've been a total ass and fool. Will you give me another chance?"

A smile crept onto Kerra's face. "I believe you taught me a certain phrase, *Toujours Pret, Always Ready.* I will always believe in you, always be ready to support and love you. It's up to you to decide to always be ready to trust yourself and me."

Dustin lifted Kerra from the floor, and kissed her with all the love he could express.

EPILOGUE
November, 2011

"I have a special place I'd like to take you tonight," Dustin told Kerra as they sat together on Saturday afternoon at the beach and holding hands. The weather was now cooler. Seventies during the day and 50's at night. But sunsets still painted the sky.

"Oh, and where would that be?"

"Do you like Ferris wheels?"

"I do. Why?"

"Well, we once had our old Miracle Strip Amusement Park that was taken down a few years ago. The Ferris wheel has been brought back to the new amusement park near the city pier. I thought it would be romantic to ride to the top and watch tonight's full moon create a lighted path across the gulf. Mom and Dad use to leave the dance at a place called the Hangout that was destroyed years ago by a hurricane and go to the Ferris wheel on full moon nights. She said they fell in love over and over again. And that was as close as an everyday person could come to touching the moon.

"I would love that," Kerra said, as she lifted Dustin's hand and kissed the top of it.

"I love you Dustin Brites."

"And I love you Kerra Masters. You've opened places in my heart I believed no one could ever reach again."

"I'm glad. And you've done the same for me. I suppose we are two very fortunate people."

After sunset, Dustin went home to change and then returned to the cottage for Kerra. She scooted close to him in his beloved pickup truck as they made their way to the Ferris wheel's new location.

"Hi, George. How's the evening going for you?" Dustin asked as he purchased tickets from the young man at the entrance gate. "I'm good Dus. I'm looking forward to that emergency ride-a-long you promised me."

"Next week. I'll see you."

Dustin took Kerra's hand and led her to the Ferris wheel where riders were disembarking one chair at a time. When the last person was gone, the ride operator opened the protective lock to a chair and held it open for Kerra and Dustin to enter. Once they were seated and the lock was secured in place, the operator put the Ferris wheel in motion.

"I haven't been on one of these in years," Kerra said. "This is wonderful. Look at all the stars. And oh my gosh, *that moon!*"

After the first full rotation, the Ferris wheel stopped at the very top.

"Look at that!" Kerra exclaimed. "I don't think I've ever seen a night so beautiful. The light from the moon makes the water look like it has a rippling glass path. And the stars look like diamonds dancing above it. I expect to see an angel appear!"

"I'm sure there's an angel, actually more than one, out there. But *you* are my special angel tonight and every night hereafter, Miss Kerra Masters. That is if you will accept this."

Dustin held out a purple velvet box and opened it. "It's my mom's. Dad gave it to her at the top of this Ferris wheel almost forty years ago."

"Oh, Dustin. I'm speechless. And *YES, YES !* I want to be your special angel, and only if it's forever. I'm so honored to accept your mom's ring."

Dustin called down to the Ferris wheel operator. "NOW HANK!"

Suddenly the old song from 1957 by Bobby Helms, *You Are My Special Angel*, played through the loud speakers. Dustin held Kerra and kissed her passionately.

When the Ferris wheel stopped, Shay was standing with Maxie and Hugh outside the gate. Sarah and Jason were together holding hands. Other fire and rescue crew members were also there. Everyone was smiling, clapping, and waiting to congratulate the newly engaged couple.

Kerra looked up at Dustin. "You planned all this didn't you?"

"Well, maybe, with some help. And I even called your mom and dad to ask permission."

"You are something else, Dustin Brites, my hero and love of my life."

Kerra looked towards Maxie, who gave her that sly grin, and toward Hugh who was beaming.

"I might get all those chairs filled yet around Mother's dining room table!" Maxie said.

Shay ran to Kerra and Dustin and wrapped his arms around both of them as tight as he could. Then he stood back. "Miss Kerra, after you and Dad marry, do I get to call you Mom?"

"Kerra looked at Dustin, then Maxie and Hugh. Everyone nodded yes.

"Absolutely Shay! Absolutely! I will be honored to be called mom, because it is the most important word in the world next to dad."

Shay moved between Dustin and Kerra and took hold of their hands. His smile made the night warmer. As everyone strolled slowly away from the Ferris wheel, something pulled Dustin's attention toward the merry-go-round. He could swear that Gloria was smiling and waving from her favorite carousel horse. And nearby were five familiar Soldiers each holding up a beer in a toast. No matter what anyone else could ever say, Dustin believed, smiled in return, and quietly whispered, *THANK YOU.*

If you know a veteran and family that can use support, please contact your local Vet Center.

Veterans Discuss Readjustment. **Vet Centers** offer a wide range of services to **Veterans** and their families at 300 community-based **Vet Center** locations.

www.vetcenter.va.gov

Bay County Vet Center

3109 Minnesota Avenue Suite 101

Lynn Haven, Fl 32405

850-522-6102

Made in the USA
Monee, IL
21 October 2021